"We might as well acknowledge that two single people working in the same office are going to be teased until people realize we're just friends."

Noah was surprised she had the guts to say it, but it was true. People had been trying to set him up on dates since the day his wife had died. Beth Brennan was the hot topic of gossip right now, and he would be mentioned in the same breath...for a while.

"Even if we ignore it, they probably won't stop until one of us starts to see someone," Beth said ruefully.

"It'll have to be you," he said dryly. "My daughter is the only woman in my life."

Beth sighed very unprofessionally. "I hate to date."

She looked so genuinely distressed that a chuckle escaped Noah's lips.

"Hey!" She frowned at his laughter. "That's going to cost you. Until I find Mr. Right, I might just act as if I don't mind the teasing. What do you think of that?" she challenged, mischief in her eyes.

She didn't *mind* if they were linked together? Noah was in big trouble....

Books by Patt Marr

Love Inspired

Angel in Disguise #98
Man of Her Dreams #289
Promise of Forever #350

PATT MARR

has a friend who says she reminds him of a car that's either zooming along in the fast lane or sitting on the shoulder, out of gas. Her family says he's dead right. At age twenty, she had a B.S. in business education, a handsome, good-hearted husband and a sweet baby girl. Since then, Patt has had a precious baby boy, earned an M.A. in counseling, worked a lifetime as a high school educator, cooked big meals for friends, attended a zillion basketball games where her husband coached and her son played. She has also enjoyed many years of church music, children's ministries, drama and television production—often working with her grown-up daughter.

During down time, Patt reads romance, eats too many carbs, watches too many movies and sleeps way too little. She's been blessed with terrific children-in-law, two darling granddaughters, two loving grandsons, many wonderful friends, a great church and a chance to write love stories about people who love God as much as she does.

PROMISE OF FOREVER

PATT MARR

Steeple
Hill®

Published by Steeple Hill Books™

STEEPLE HILL BOOKS

Steeple
Hill®

ISBN 0-373-81264-7

PROMISE OF FOREVER

Copyright © 2006 by Patt Marr

www.SteepleHill.com

Printed in U.S.A.

For I know the plans I have for you.
They are plans for good and not for
disaster, to give you a hope and a future.
—*Jeremiah* 29:11

Heartfelt appreciation for help with
this book goes to my cousin Paul Lawrence,
for expert critique; my daughter J. Marr,
for endless encouragement; my son and
daughter-in-law, Dane and Carla Marr,
for providing the prototype of the character,
Kendra; and Beth Elwood, R.N.,
for technical advice.

I dedicate this story to a woman of
unshakable faith, my dear friend, Sue Lemmon.

Prologue

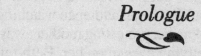

Beverly Hills, California—April

For one moment, Dr. Beth Brennan felt as if she soared on invisible wings, floating on the approval of her entire family and the Brennan Medical Clinic staff. Well-wishers thronged about her, congratulating her for finishing her residency and becoming the new clinic pediatrician.

In the next moment, her mother's manic rage came out of nowhere, and she launched into the most outrageous of all of her tantrums. The room went silent as Deborah Brennan's illness took center stage.

Everyone here was associated with the clinic in some way. Most of them had been guests in Beth's parents' home. They knew her mother as a vibrant, elegant hostess, not this vicious tyrant, but her manic behavior wouldn't be the family secret anymore.

It shouldn't have come to this, not with seven doctors in the Brennan family. Not one of them, including Beth, had the guts to stand up to her mother and make her get the help she needed. If they had, there wouldn't be an audience watching her dad and uncle drag her protesting mother away.

With so many pitying eyes upon her, Beth felt paralyzed. She wanted to leave, but her feet wouldn't move.

A tall man in blue scrubs—a man about her own age with close-cropped dark hair and intense brown eyes—took her elbow. "Your grandfather sent me to get you, Dr. Brennan."

Beth was a veteran at fighting her own battles, but, just this once, retreat seemed like a better idea.

They didn't talk on the way to her grandfather's office. Another time she would have paid more attention to the man's chiseled good looks and muscular build. She might have shrugged away from his hand on her elbow and made some joke about knowing the way to her grandfather's office as well as every inch of this building. But his steadying presence offered the perfect amount of comfort without pity.

"Who are you?" she asked.

"I'm Noah," he answered, opening the door to her grandfather's office.

"Thank you, Noah," her grandfather said.

The man nodded and shut the door behind her.

Noah. Sometime, she would thank him.

"Come in, Beth. Sit here beside me." Her handsome, white-haired grandfather patted the burgundy leather sofa.

She snuggled close, glad they were there for each other. Grandpa had been the anchor in her life, the one person she could always count on.

"How's my favorite granddaughter?"

His only granddaughter. It was an old joke, but she usually played along. Not today. She leaned her head on his shoulder.

"It wasn't quite the celebration we'd hoped for, was it, darling?" He leaned his head against hers.

"Did I tell you how nice you look?"

He might have, but today the credit for her looks belonged to Mom.

Normally, Beth washed her low-maintenance short blond hair, applied facial cream with sunblock, gave her eyelashes a dab of mascara, and she was good to go.

Today, her mother had insisted on the whole beauty salon treatment…styled hair, major makeup, painted fingernails, the works. The only thing the professionals left natural was the color of her eyes—a light brown they'd raved about and called dark honey.

She'd looked forward to this day for as long as she could remember. It should have been a happy time.

"I don't know what it was that made your mother lose control this time, but if it wasn't one thing, it could have been another."

That was true. Anything could trigger one of her mother's episodes. As a child, she'd learned to stay out of the way.

"What's this?" Grandpa said, pointing to a large red blotch on her sleeve. "Cranberry punch?"

She shrugged. It didn't matter. The taupe silk suit, the matching pumps, her grandmother's pearls—they'd all been chosen by her mother as perfect for the day. None of it was Beth's style. She'd worn it to keep the peace, though a lot of good it had done.

From now on, she would wear what she liked.

"Beth, darling, it was twenty years ago that we walked the building site for the clinic together. Remember?"

Of course she did. "We drew on the ground where your office would be."

"And where yours would be. You said you were going to be a doctor like Grandpa."

He loved taking the credit for her career choice,

and she loved acknowledging it. "You put the idea in my mind. You gave me the doctor kit and pretended to be my patient."

"Have you been sorry, darling?"

"Never. I love medicine. I wouldn't want to do anything else."

"It was a thrill for me, getting to introduce you today." He patted her hand. "Call it an old man's dream, but I've always wanted my children and my grandchildren to practice medicine under one roof."

"Grandpa, you've wanted a medical dynasty," she teased.

"That *is* what people say, isn't it?" he asked with a chuckle.

"And I'm proud to be part of it."

"People will always talk about us, Beth—sometimes with respect, sometimes with spite. With a family like ours, people look for every flaw. They pounce on a juicy piece of gossip and chew the living daylights out of it. After what happened today, it's going to be worse. I think it would be better if you weren't here for a while. The gossips would make your life miserable, and I can't have that."

He had to be kidding. "Dealing with gossip is part of our life. It comes and goes. You taught me that."

He nodded. "And when this latest wave goes, you'll begin your work here. I won't have your first memories of working with me tainted by your mother's mania."

"You think I can't handle a little gossip?"

"I'm sure you could handle anything, but I see no reason to test your endurance, not when it's so easily avoided."

"What about Keith Crabtree? He's expecting me to replace him in two weeks."

"This is Keith's idea. You know what a private person he's always been. He came to me, seconds after the hullabaloo. It was his idea to give you a break."

"A 'break'?"

"Keith has known you since you were his patient. When you did your internship in peds, he suggested you as his replacement. We want you here, but we know this place. Both of us think a delay is in order."

She wasn't going to have any say in this? "How do you explain this 'break' to all those people who just heard I was coming aboard?" she asked, standing, the better to pace the room and deal with the ball of anger forming in her stomach.

"We didn't announce a particular date when you were to join us, so it's no problem. Take the summer off, love. Come back in a few months, and we'll get you started off right."

"And what will people think when Keith doesn't retire?"

"Nothing. No one knew he planned to retire. Not even his own staff. He wanted to leave without fanfare. The staff thinks you're starting an office of your own. They'll merely think you're taking your time about it."

"It seems the two of you have this figured out." Technically, Grandpa was her boss and had the right to make decisions for his staff, but it felt as if he was treating her like a child.

"Beth, don't be upset. This is for your own good. Now, tell me, where have you dreamed of going—Europe, the Orient, somewhere in the tropics? You can go anywhere. My treat. Make a dream come true."

She only had one dream, and that was on the third floor of this building.

He stood, pulled her into his arms and patted her back. "It's going to be fine, Beth."

She hugged him hard, hoping he would feel how much she loved him…had always loved him.

"Let me know where you want to go. I'll set it up. I want you to have the best time of your life." He kept his arm around her as he walked her to the door. "We'll see you soon."

He shut the door, and she was alone in the hall.

No, not alone. The tall man in blue scrubs leaned against the wall—not so near the office that he could have heard what went on, but as if he might be waiting. For her? Or was he the next to see Grandpa?

Pushing off the wall, his serious face softened as he said, "Are you okay?"

She must not look it, or he wouldn't have asked. But she wasn't going to share her heartache with a stranger, especially not one who seemed to have everything going for him, and her own life had just fallen apart.

Tall and lean, he moved toward her with the effortless strength of an athlete, but it was his eyes that drew her to him. Intelligence shone from those brown eyes, and dark eyebrows winged across his masculine brow. There was a small scar across his cheekbone and another across his angular jaw. His nose had been quite perfect before it was broken. None of the flaws were new, nor did they take away from his good looks.

If he was aware of his appeal, she couldn't tell it, and if she were better at trusting good-looking men, she would believe what his eyes seemed to say— that his concern was genuine, and it was all for her.

"Am I okay?" she repeated. She would be. She had to believe that. "Yes, and thanks for asking. I'm on my way out." That was true in more ways than one.

"Can I walk you to your car?" he said, his voice naturally deep.

"Have you been waiting for me?" Why would he do that? "Did my grandfather ask you to do that, too?"

"Yes, I've been waiting, and no, he didn't ask me."

"Why did you?"

He shrugged as if he wasn't sure and looked away.

"I could use the company," she said. If being with him was as comforting now as it had been, she definitely could.

They walked in silence, passing staring groups. Some would have stopped her, but not with this guy beside her. He had a forbidding look that kept them at bay. What was his name?

She pointed out her car, a congratulatory gift from her parents, though her mother would have been the one to choose it. Beth thought the tan-gray color was blah. Her mother said taupe was classy and Beth had no taste.

"Nice car," he said quietly.

He probably meant "expensive car." The luxury convertible wasn't her style, but then, she had no taste.

He watched her settle behind the wheel, the way a pro bodyguard would. Meeting him was the only good thing in this horrible day.

"Drive carefully," he said, his face full of concern.

"I want to thank you..." She searched for his name again and came up blank. "I don't know when I'll have another chance."

He smiled, and her heart seemed to turn over.

"I work here, Dr. Brennan. We'll see each other soon."

It wasn't the Brennan way to confide family affairs, but she couldn't help saying, "No, I won't be returning, not any time in the foreseeable future."

He looked shocked. "You're not leaving because...?" He stopped as if it wasn't his business and he'd overstepped by saying what he had.

"Actually, I'm a little confused about the reason I'm leaving. I just know I am." She smiled so she wouldn't cry.

"But you'll be back."

She couldn't confirm that, and she couldn't let this gorgeous guy see her break down. It was better to drive away with some of her pride intact.

Chapter One

New York, New York—September, seventeen months later

Autumn in New York City was Beth's favorite time of year. It was only her second season here, but it seemed as if the leaves were falling earlier. She crunched through a clump on the sidewalk, walking back to work after lunch.

Because it was her birthday, she'd just split a delicious mile-high pastrami sandwich with a friend and indulged in her very own piece of chocolate-ripple cheesecake. With each lush, creamy bite, she'd told herself it wasn't so bad, turning thirty.

Her lunch buddy was a doctor who volunteered part-time at Manhattan Free Clinic. Beth volunteered there, too, but full-time. As long as she was careful with her grandmother's trust-fund money, she could afford to work without pay.

She loved working at the clinic, mostly because they were so glad to have her. No one hinted that she was on the staff because she was somebody's relative. No one suggested that she might not be able to handle the job.

She'd come here at her brother Ry's suggestion. He knew about Manhattan Free Clinic from his years working as a New York City paramedic. Since she hadn't known how long it would take for her to find a new dream, she hadn't wanted to sign a contract anywhere.

The work was a hybrid of ER medicine and private family practice. If and when she decided to leave, she would be taking more experience than she would have gained working the same amount of time at Brennan Medical Clinic.

Home was a tiny apartment on the Upper East Side, close enough to Central Park for her daily run. She'd wanted to live near the clinic in lower Manhattan, but her brother said she would appreciate a quiet neighborhood to go home to.

He'd been right. The city was a noisy place, with millions of people on the move. The infinite variety of sights and sounds had been a culture shock, but she'd grown to love it all. If it weren't for missing Ry and Meg, Beth could stay here indefinitely.

Her cell phone rang, and the caller ID said Ry was about to wish her a happy birthday.

"Ry!" she said, answering with a smile. "I was just thinking about you."

"How's the birthday girl?"

"Lovin' New York, missin' you and Meg."

"How did you like my present this morning?"

"Very much!" she said, laughing. "Thank you!"

A trio of his buddies had shown up at the clinic to sing "Happy Birthday." The best-looking one asked her to dinner tonight and begged her to go since Ry was footing the bill. She'd thought, why not? It wasn't as if she'd met anyone who mattered, and she didn't want to be alone on her thirtieth birthday.

"They called after they'd seen you," Ry said, laughing. "Your date for the night thanked *me*. He said you were the most attractive doc he'd ever seen."

"It must have been my yellow sneakers. They draw men like flies." She caught a glimpse of herself in a store window. Her yellow sneakers, blue scrubs and navy hoody sweatshirt with the New York Yankees logo made quite the fashion statement.

Her new hair cut was cool, though. The uneven blond length was more of a frame for her face than a style. The stylist had said he only gave this cut to pretty women with fine features, but he'd also said she should have permanent, tattooed eyeliner and lipstick. That wouldn't be happening. She just wasn't that trendy.

"Have you heard from the rest of the family?"

"Not yet. Grandpa will call. Dad might, but I don't expect to hear from Mom."

"It's not just you, Beth. Since she moved in with Aunt Jackie, she's shut herself off from the rest of the family," he said comfortingly.

"I ask myself, how could the things that happened on one day tear Mom apart from her family so drastically?"

Ry cleared his throat. "You're not going to like this, but I ask myself that every time I place a call to you a continent away."

That stung. "I talk to Grandpa. He calls, I call him." She'd gotten over her hurt feelings long ago.

"What do you tell Grandpa about coming back and working at the clinic?"

"That I'm still looking for a new dream."

"What's wrong with the old one?" he said, reproof in his voice.

Reproof? From the family rebel? "Isn't that the pot calling the kettle black? *You* don't plan to work at the clinic when you get your M.D."

"Right, but I never wanted to. You *always* did."

"Give me that phone." That was Meg's voice in the background. "You don't nag a person on her birthday."

Beth grinned. Her favorite brother and her lifelong best friend made a great pair.

"Beth, don't mind him," Meg said, just as sassy as ever. "I wish you were here so we could celebrate your birthday at the beach, like we used to do."

They ended the call as Beth neared the clinic. A chilly breeze blew through her hair, and she thought about home. It would be summer-hot there and very dry. The leaves wouldn't change color until close to Thanksgiving, and, if it had been a very dry year, they would just go brown. Here, the trees were a glorious riot of red, orange and gold.

She'd learned to love the changing seasons. Each one made her more aware of her Creator. She'd been a brand-new Christian when she'd arrived a year ago last spring, but she'd studied the Word and knew Him much better now. He'd become her friend, someone she could talk to any time, any place—even now on the streets of New York.

Father God, it's my birthday. You've given me the best presents anyone could have—a relationship with You, satisfying work, good health, friends—everything, actually, but a man of my own...and a baby!

I'm ready for them, Lord—the man and the baby! I'm more than ready. I won't say I'm desperate, because no self-respecting woman admits that, but I can't fool You. You know my heart.

Beth's last patient of the day was a tough eleven-year-old kid with a long gash on his arm. She sutured the wound while the boy's mother paced the small examining room and complained that he was nothing but a gangbanger, just like his brother.

The woman reminded Beth of her own mother—far less cultured, but just as hateful. In moments like these, it was hard to remember that a Christian prayed first and reacted second. The instinct to stand up for this boy was strong, but God could do more for him than she ever could.

Father, you know the need. Help this child and his family. Please silence this woman's words. If you want help from me, I'm your willing servant.

The boy threw his mom a cocky smile. It might have been sheer bravado, but his mother threw up her hands and stormed out of the room.

Wow! If that was an answer to prayer, it came with the speed of light.

"So, tell me, Stevie, how did you get this cut?"

Beth said, praying again, this time for words that might make a difference in the boy's life.

"Me and my brother was practicing fighting."

"With real knives? Isn't that kind of dangerous?"

"My brother says you gotta keep it real if you're gonna be ready when somebody comes at you with the real thing."

What a philosophy! She would make sure he saw the staff social worker before he got out of here. Not only was it her duty to report a wound like this, somebody should think of this kid's safety.

"Am I gonna have a scar?" He sounded hopeful.

"Not unless you want one. I'm good at this." She hadn't been much older than Stevie when her grandfather had begun teaching her suturing techniques.

"Scars are kind of cool," the boy said, watching her work. "You're kind of cool, too, even if you smell like baby puke."

"You don't like my perfume?"

He grinned at her little joke.

"I was about to change into fresh scrubs when you came in here, bleeding all over the place."

"Is that my blood on your shoes?"

"Probably."

"How come you wear yellow shoes?"

"They make me happy."

"Aren't you mad that I got blood on 'em? It made my mom real mad when I got blood on her towel."

She smiled, hoping he would see the love of Jesus in her eyes. That's what she was here for. "Do I look mad?"

He smiled back. "No, you look pretty. I think I could go for you."

Maybe she'd overdone the smile.

"I dig blond chicks, even if you are kind of old."

Stevie needed a little work on his pickup lines.

"You've got pretty eyes."

That was better.

"I never seen anybody with that eye color. They're kind of gold or brown or somethin'. And you got long eyelashes. Are you seeing anybody?"

Kids hated when they were treated like kids. If she could hang in here and talk to him as if he were an adult, there might be an opening to talk about Jesus. "I'm still single, Stevie. How about you?"

"I'm not with anybody either. You wanna go out some time, Doc?"

There it was. "I might if we went to church. You wanna take me to church?"

"Nah. I mean, like on a real date, like a movie."

"Sorry, but I can't go on real dates with my patients."

"Oh, sure. I understand."

"But the invitation to church still holds." She described the store-front church near the clinic and their cool program for kids.

"I might try it some time," Stevie said, maybe to please. "You know, you're a really good doctor. The best I've ever seen."

One of the male volunteers popped his head in. "Doctor, we're having your surprise birthday party in the lounge now. Can I finish up with this patient, and can you go act surprised?"

She glanced at Stevie, caught his quick look of disappointment and said, "Would you mind bringing a couple of pieces of cake in here?"

"No problem."

"Stevie, I want you to talk to our social worker for a few minutes, and then we'll have cake together. Okay?"

"No way! I ain't seeing no social worker." Stevie scooted off the table, fast as a wink. She grabbed for him as he bolted for the door, but he was gone.

It was the end of the day before Beth made it to the staff lounge to sit down. She didn't mind that she was alone or that cake crumbs were all that was left of her party. It was good to have a quiet spot to check her voice mail before heading home.

She plopped down on the secondhand sofa, put

her feet on the rickety coffee table and found the message she'd hoped for. Grandpa had called.

She called him back, and he answered quickly, as if he'd been waiting. "Happy birthday, darling."

"Thank you, Grandpa. What are you doing this fine autumn day?"

"Looking at flight schedules. If you're not ever going to come home, I'm coming to see you."

Beth's heart skipped a beat. She would love that.

"I thought I'd like to see the fall colors along the Hudson River. I haven't been to New York in decades."

She couldn't believe it. "This is great, Grandpa! We'll have to see the sights and do all the tourist things."

"Maybe not all," he said chuckling. "I'm not much of a walker anymore."

Despite the age-related quaver in his voice, he sounded so vital and strong that she forgot his body wasn't.

"I miss you, Beth. I'll never forgive myself for the decision that made you go so far away."

They had talked this to death, but once again she said, "If you were wrong, I was just as wrong to get offended. I've been at such peace here, that it must have been the right thing. Maybe I wasn't ready to work at BMC; maybe I needed this time away to learn what makes me happy. For sure, I tried too hard to please Mom, Dad, you, the whole family."

"Trying to please is part of life, but it can't *be* your life. Now that you know what makes you happy, can you be happy back here?"

"At the clinic?"

"You don't have to work at BMC. There are free clinics in the L.A. area if that's your passion or if it's too much for you to work with the family."

Too much for her? Running a peds office at Brennan Medical would be a piece of cake compared to her work at a free clinic.

"What would it take to get you back, Beth?"

If she hadn't found a new dream in all this time, was it God's plan for her to go back? Could she work there?

"You belong here, darling."

She didn't believe that anymore. How could she convince him? "Grandpa, you've brought together some of the brightest, most experienced doctors in L.A. They've earned the right to practice in an exclusive group, and they value BMC's prestigious address. My chief credential is that I'm your granddaughter, and I could care less that our patients are rich or famous. I don't belong there!"

"You're the future, Beth. Of course you belong."

"I would only be a disappointment to you, or, worse, an embarrassment."

"Never!"

"Not even if I wore a frog on my head?"

A loud guffaw had her pulling the phone from her ear. "I believe that's *my* traditional New Year's Eve hat."

It was. "But I wear funny hats in the office any time I want to, not just like the family does on New Year's Eve. I collect yellow sneakers in different styles and wear a pair every day. I'm rather eccentric, Grandpa, and I love it. In New York, nobody notices, but, if gossip about the family was an issue for you a year and a half ago, think what it would be like if I were there now."

There was such silence that Beth thought they'd lost their phone connection.

"Grandpa…?"

"I'm here. I'm thinking."

Maybe she'd finally made her point. Shouldn't that make her feel better than she did? She hated arguing with Grandpa.

"Beth, the last time we talked, I said I'd like to fly you home, first class, and I would have a brand-new car waiting for you. Do you remember what you said?"

"I said if material things mattered, I wouldn't be working as a volunteer at a free clinic." She felt almost as insulted now, repeating the words, as she had, saying them the first time. She was above taking a bribe.

"Well, what if I said the car that would be waiting for you could be one of those new VW convertibles?"

"A Beetle?" She loved those fun little cars.

"It could be yellow to match your shoes. Imagine it, Beth. Your yellow VW parked in the physicians' lot, surrounded by every luxury car on the market. It would stand out like a dandelion in an arrangement of roses and announce to the world that the clinic's new pediatrician was a person who thought for herself and knew what she wanted. What do you think?"

She thought she needed a tissue. Tears trickled down her cheeks. She had just one thing left to say.

"I'm coming home, Grandpa."

Noah McKnight admired his daughter's drawing of Brennan Medical Clinic one last time before taking it to work. At the top was her trademark rainbow and Welcome Dr. Brennan, printed in crayon. For a second-grader who'd just turned seven, Kendi had produced a masterpiece, or at least he thought so.

"Daddy, do you think Dr. Brennan will like my welcome sign?"

"Like it? Kendi, she'll love it!" He lifted her high and kissed her forehead, loving the feel of her long blond hair swishing against his face.

He lowered her to the counter stool so she could supervise. Carefully, he rolled her drawing into a cylinder, making sure it would travel unwrinkled. If he didn't do the job right, she would tell him about it.

She sat on her knees, leaning over the counter, keeping a watchful eye. Her beautiful hair swung down, covering part of her face.

"You did a nice job of brushing your hair," he said. A compliment might soften his daughter's strong will.

"I know," she said, matter-of-factly. She took being beautiful for granted, just as she took being tall for her age and right-handed.

"How about wearing one of those new barrettes?"

"No," she said, shaking that blond mane.

"They're yellow."

"I love yellow!" she said with a sunny smile.

Like he didn't know that? "I could French braid your hair." He was getting better at it.

But she just shook her head, closing the discussion as only she could. Kendi never sassed or was hateful, but she had decided opinions on how most things should be, and there wasn't a wishy-washy bone in her body. If her mother had been that strong, they might still be a family of three.

"Do you think Dr. Brennan will like the rainbow?"

"She'll love the rainbow."

"How do you know that, Daddy?"

"Dr. Brennan is a pediatrician, just like your pediatrician, Dr. Marsha. You know how much Dr. Marsha likes the things you make for her."

"Yep, she does. And Dr. Crabtree liked his goodbye picture."

"Yep," he agreed, though he wasn't that sure. In the two years Noah had worked as Keith Crabtree's office nurse, the man had rarely shown enthusiasm or genuine interest in others. It was his reputation for thoroughness, not his personality, that kept his patient roster full.

"Is Dr. Brennan pretty, Daddy?"

"Does that matter?"

"Nope, but is she?"

"I only met her once, and it was a long time ago." A year and a half was a long time, measured by Kendi's standards. They'd buried her mother six months before that.

He remembered Beth Brennan better than he admitted, though. When she was introduced as Dr. Crabtree's replacement, she'd been radiant, happy and so attractive that he'd wondered what it was going to be like working in the close quarters of their office.

Later, when he'd walked with her to her grand-father's office, and, later still, to her car, he hadn't been thinking how she looked, just how she must feel. Ragged emotion showed on her face, and he'd wished he could help.

"Does Dr. Brennan like little girls?"

"Sure. And little boys, too."

"Is Dr. Brennan married?"

"I don't know." She hadn't been when she'd first planned to take Crabtree's place, but she could be now.

"Well, if she's not, maybe Dr. Brennan could be your girlfriend."

Whoa! Where did that come from? He hadn't had a girlfriend since he'd met Kendi's mother, and he didn't want one now. "No, Kendra, Dr. Brennan can't be my girlfriend."

"You called me Kendra."

"That's your name."

"Yeah, but you never call me Kendra unless you're kind of mad at me."

Did he really do that? "But I love your name. Mommy gave it to you."

"Why can't Dr. Brennan be your girlfriend?"

"Because she's my boss."

"Why can't she be your girlfriend *and* your boss?"

"It's not a good idea."

"Why not?"

Okay, he was thirty; she was seven. He should be able to end a conversation. Before Merrilee died, he could have. As the only one left to love Kendi, it was difficult to be hard on her, even a little bit.

He leaned across the counter and tweaked her nose playfully. "Remember when Justin was your boyfriend?"

"Dad-dee! William is my boyfriend!"

"I know. Was Justin mad when you started liking William?"

Kendi giggled. "Yep. He wouldn't talk to me for a whole day."

"That's the way it is with grown-ups, too. If Dr. Beth was my girlfriend, and I got a *new* girlfriend, she might get mad, and I would have to find a *new* job."

"I like new jobs."

"Yeah, well, you don't always like new jobs when you're a grown-up."

"Why?" Her big blue-violet eyes were glued to his.

Usually, he tried to break things down so she could understand, but this lesson could wait. He knew just the thing to make those eyes glaze with indifference.

"Kendi, when you have to find a new job, you lose your seniority, your retirement benefits, the relationship you've developed with colleagues and the opportunity to continue working in an environment you initially chose. You have to begin the job search all over again—networking with former coworkers about openings, interviewing potential employers, assessing whether this work is a good fit for your skills and temperament. You might never find a position you like as well."

"Daddy?"

"Yes, Kendra?"

"Can we have hot dogs for dinner?"

Chapter Two

Beverly Hills, California—October, one month later

There it was, the ultimate trophy: a parking space of her own. The flat piece of metal read Dr. E. Brennan, which meant the sign maker didn't know she was Beth, not Elizabeth, but that didn't matter—not when she'd spent a year and a half depending on the New York subway system, taxis and her own two feet to get around.

Beth wheeled her new yellow Beetle convertible into the space between two luxury cars. Grandpa had been right. Compared to the other vehicles in the BMC physicians' parking area, her VW stood out like a happy child at a convention of bankers. It didn't fit in any more than she did, but they were both here to stay.

It had been humbling to see how willingly Grandpa had agreed to the changes she'd wanted in her office, and he hadn't been exaggerating about Keith Crabtree wanting to leave without fanfare.

She'd met with Keith after hours in his office and worked out the transition, but she hadn't greeted the staff she would inherit. The receptionist—a young woman in her early twenties—was new to her. One of Keith's nurses had been there when Beth was a child and a patient herself. Her other nurse was a widower who'd begun working at BMC when he'd needed better hours to raise his daughter alone.

When Keith mentioned his name, Noah McKnight, Beth couldn't put a face with the name, but she sincerely hoped the man had a good sense of humor. She hadn't realized there was anyone named Noah on her staff when she chose the theme of her new office decor. It was such an odd coincidence that she'd considered changing the theme, but it was exactly what she wanted, and her decorator had already placed custom orders.

Grandpa said if Noah had a problem with it, they would transfer him to another doctor's office. Beth hoped it didn't come to that. No one should lose his job or have his life rearranged because she was here.

High overhead, huge palm fronds swished in

the warm fall breeze. The sky was California-blue without a cloud in sight. Beth raised her face to the sun and told herself this was the beginning of a great new life.

The people inside that classy glass-and-stucco building might scoff at the latest Brennan grandchild coming aboard, but she was well-trained, hard-working, resourceful and unafraid. Nothing could ruffle her composure. Nothing could make her doubt herself.

Or could it?

She must be more nervous than she wanted to admit, but was it any wonder? The Brennan family reputation was a heavy load to bear. There were people inside who would love to see her fall on her face, and that was not just paranoia talking.

She tossed her car keys into her tote bag and slung the tote over her shoulder. From the car's back seat, she gathered up a floral arrangement, two big gift bags and a smaller one. Arriving this early, she hoped to have her gifts on the desks of her staff when they arrived.

Stepping briskly, she headed toward the front entrance, as nervous as an intern on her first day. Today she would be working without a net, with no attending physician to consult and no colleague close by. In her office, she was on her own as never before.

On her own? That was old Beth thinking. She knew better than that. She could pray anytime.

Lord, I need you today.

It wasn't much of a prayer, but a flood of confidence swept over her, surprising her with its immediacy and power. Before she was a Christian, she might have called it mind over matter or something equally indefinable, but she knew better now. The effect of faith on the human body was real.

Noah McKnight jogged from the employee parking lot toward the BMC staff entrance and took the back stairs, two at a time, hurrying to reach the office and get his daughter's sign pinned to the bulletin board before Beth Brennan arrived. This time his daughter's artwork would get the appreciation it deserved.

He rounded the landing and started up the next flight, grateful for this chance to stretch his legs. He'd been a nurse before Kendi was born, but he'd only been a health nut since Merrilee had died and he'd realized he was all Kendi had. If something happened to him, what would become of her?

When he thought of his baby being raised in a foster home, it felt like there was a giant claw in his stomach. He knew there were good people who raised kids for the state, and he'd known some, but he'd taken off on his own as soon as he could. Merrilee's foster situation hadn't been much better.

If there was a God, he would get to raise Kendi himself, but he hadn't seen much reason to count on help from above. Merrilee had, and look where it got her.

Sometimes he missed the feeling that God was in control. If he were still a praying man, he would pray that things would go better today than he feared they would. Keith Crabtree's sudden departure had been a shock to the staff, but a terrible blow to Mona Fitz, the senior nurse in the office. The doc and Mona worked together for over thirty years.

They'd all known Keith would be gone, but not for good. A couple of weeks before, he'd said he was taking the first week in October to go fishing. That wasn't unusual. Keith often went fishing.

When Keith gave them all the same week off—with pay—Noah should have realized something was up. Keith had called it an early Christmas gift, but he'd never made such a generous gesture.

On that last day, Keith's face had been void of emotion when he told them he'd just seen his last patient…ever. Beth Brennan was back in town and would be his replacement. He shook their hands and was gone.

Mona fell apart, sobbing and threatening retribution against the Brennans and their "spoiled princess" for forcing Keith out of a job. She wouldn't be consoled by Vanessa, their young receptionist, or listen to reason from himself. The Brennans weren't to blame because Keith wanted to retire. Anyone could see he'd lost his zest for the job.

This past week, Noah had spent a lot of time worrying about Mona's attitude and whether Beth Brennan would know her stuff. Had she gotten her position because of her name? Would she be a powder puff and let Mona run the show, or would the two of them lock horns and he'd have to referee?

In all this time, would Beth have changed as much as he had? He'd worked through the stages of grieving, and it seemed like he had his sense of humor back.

Thinking, worrying, wondering what Mona would do today, Noah opened the stairwell door and stopped in his tracks. Stepping out of the elevator was Dr. Beth Brennan. Would she remember him?

The new doc smiled as if seeing him just made her day. It was no doubt mere friendliness, but Noah's heart rate picked up as if it were more. Of course, he had also just run up a double flight of stairs.

"You're Noah, aren't you?"

"I didn't think you would remember me." He was unreasonably pleased that she had.

"Remember you?" A frown crossed her pretty face.

"We met…" If she didn't remember, maybe he shouldn't remind her of that bad day. "It was a while ago."

"But I usually have a very good memory for names and faces." She studied his face intently.

"Don't worry about it. We barely met. But how did you know my name?" He sounded like a single guy talking to a single woman. That wasn't like him. He never thought of himself as single.

"The scrubs," she answered, glancing at his work attire. "Since you're in scrubs, and I've learned that BMC only has one male nurse, you must be Noah."

That was him all right. Around here, he was one of a kind. Some men might have liked that, but not him. If the regular hours of this job weren't better for Kendi, he would be back, doing the job he loved in a hospital ER.

"I've lived in scrubs for so long," she said, "that it seems strange to show up for work in street clothes."

Just then he noticed what she was wearing, right down to the yellow sneakers that matched her yellow shirt. Her khaki pants fit just right, and her only jewelry was a practical watch. There was nothing about the doc that shouted "spoiled princess."

If Mona had anything to complain about, it would be how young Beth Brennan looked. Without her long lab coat, no one would believe she was the doctor.

"I'm Beth Brennan, in case you're as bad at remembering names as I am," she said, setting down a couple of gift bags and extending her hand. "We'll be working together."

"I know," he said, surprised at how his shortness of breath lingered on. He hadn't realized he was this out of shape. "Can I carry those bags for you, Dr. Brennan?" he asked, trying to sound natural.

"Thank you, but, please, call me Beth."

Walking side by side toward the office, he noticed that the top of her head was level with his chin, though the length of her stride matched his. Just guessing, he would say she ran or jogged regularly. Whatever she did to workout was working just fine. She was in great shape.

"I can't tell you how happy I am that you're part of my staff, Noah," she said with a secretive smile. "Without you, our office just wouldn't be complete."

Oh, no. Here he was, ready to like and respect Beth Brennan, and she had to come on to him? That stuff started soon after Merrilee's death, and it still turned him off.

They rounded a corner, and their lobby came into sight. Noah stopped dead. A week ago the lobby had looked as impersonal as every other waiting area in the clinic. The only way a person would have known it was a pediatrician's office was the presence of a little table-and-chair set and some kiddy magazines.

This morning, sunshine poured in on a child-friendly play area with pairs of elephants, tigers and zebras as chairs for the kids. Bright-colored fish darted about in a big aquarium, and on the wall was a really cute mural of Noah's ark and a big rainbow.

Okay, he got it, and he owed the doc an apology for jumping to the wrong conclusion. Grinning, he said, "I take it I'm to play the part of Noah."

"For the record," she said, looking anxious, "the decorator had placed custom orders before I realized I had a Noah on my staff. I hope you don't mind."

Her earnest explanation said a lot. Only a really good person would care about such a little thing. "How can I mind? It's not like I had to build the ark. How did you get all this done so fast?"

"Obviously, I had a lot of help. Do you like it?"

She shouldn't have had to ask. "Of course I like it! It's great!" Kendi would love it, especially that rainbow.

"There's more," Beth said, her face happy with anticipation as she unlocked the door to the office.

Noah braced himself for disaster. If she'd changed Mona's kingdom as much as she'd changed the lobby, Mona would have a fit.

But the front office was exactly as they'd left it. He almost sighed in relief.

Her soft laugh said she'd caught that. "I thought I'd better leave the front office alone."

"Good call." That was twice that she'd shown she cared about how others felt. How could Mona find fault with that?

"There are other changes, though." Beth set the flowers on the counter. He set the bags there, too, and followed her down the hall.

Opening the doors of the three exam rooms, she flipped on the lights for him to see that each room had received a quick facelift. Caricatures of a pair of happy monkeys covered the back wall of Exam Room One. Room Two hosted a pair of silly zebras, and Three had a pair of giraffes with such goofy expressions he had to laugh.

"Good! You're laughing," she said, sounding relieved.

"This is just…great!" He couldn't help being impressed. Beth Brennan had known what she wanted in her new practice and wasted no time putting it into motion.

She walked over to a brand-new stand-alone cabinet and opened it, the better for him to see inside.

The shelves were stocked with an assortment of the silliest hats and headgear he'd ever seen. They looked adult size. "Are these for Mona and me to wear?" he asked, knowing Mona Fitz would burn the place down before she learned how to have fun.

"Actually, the hats are for me, but I might share. I got the idea from our family's New Year's Eve parties where everyone wears a crazy hat."

He'd heard about those hats, and he'd been invited to the Brennans' New Year's Eve party the last two years. If Merrilee had been alive, they would have gone.

Beth chose a shiny red beret with a coiled wire toy attached to the top. "What do you think?" she asked, moving her head so the toy sprang wildly from side to side. "Do you think this will distract a little kid?"

It would certainly distract him, and she wouldn't even have to wear the hat. Man, the doc was cute. She didn't seem to be wearing any makeup, but she was so naturally pretty with those caramel-colored eyes, straight little nose and truly terrific smile, that makeup sure wasn't necessary.

"You know how difficult it is to examine kids

when they're frightened," she said. "If we're having fun, I'll get to do my job and they won't dread coming here. At least that's the plan."

"It ought to work." If anyone could pull that off, she would be the one, and if Beth knew medicine as well as she knew kids, she was going to be great.

She took the hat off and ran her hand through her sun-streaked hair as if it didn't particularly matter how it fell. He couldn't imagine many women—or men—risking a hair style that casual, but on her, it looked great.

"What did you want to be when you were a little boy?" she asked. "Choose a hat, and you're halfway there."

He was halfway there already, at least when it came to feeling at ease with his new boss. He'd assumed that she would be intelligent, kind, caring, as most peds docs were, but it was her joy of life that drew him in. He'd felt like smiling from the moment they met.

He picked up a diamond tiara with a plume of feathers attached. "My daughter would love this."

"Is she one of our patients?"

"Not yet." But she would be. Kendi needed this doc's sense of fun as badly as he did himself.

"Anytime she comes in, she can wear it, but she might surprise you. We girls don't always want to be royalty. I would have picked this one when I was little." She chose a football helmet and plunked it on her head.

"You liked to play football?" he asked, thinking how different that was from his little girl.

"Not as much as other sports, but I wanted my mother to think I was as headstrong and out of control as my brother, who did play."

"Trey Brennan, out of control?" That was an image impossible to conceive.

Laughter burst from her. "Not Trey! He would never do anything my mother disapproved of! Golf and tennis were his games. It was my brother Ry who played football."

Noah had forgotten that she had another brother. Ry Brennan, the family rebel, had been introduced at Beth's reception nearly two years ago.

"I take it that you know Trey," she said dryly.

Noah couldn't stand the guy, but he probably ought to keep his opinion of her brother to himself. "When Dr. Crabtree needed a neurological consult, he used a doctor more familiar with peds patients."

"Good! Our kids deserve somebody who's nice."

That was calling it like it was.

"Do you know my uncles?"

"Not well." Why be candid when it could only

hurt her feelings? Her womanizing uncle, Dr. Charles Brennan, was an excellent cardiologist, but the female staff had no respect for him. Her uncle Al was a brilliant orthopedic surgeon, but a patronizing, sarcastic know-it-all, as unlikable as her brother Trey.

"How about my grandfather? Do you know him?"

He knew the senior Brennan better than he was supposed to admit, so he said, "Everyone knows the chief! Your grandfather's amazing. He makes a point of knowing all of the staff. He asks about their kids and their grandkids. You can tell he suffers a lot with his arthritis, but he makes it to the office every day. He's the best."

That brought a glow to Beth's face. "He's a hard man to say no to. He can talk me into anything."

She wasn't the only one. When the chief called last week and asked Noah to keep an eye on Mona, it hadn't felt right, going behind Beth's back even if her grandfather did have her best interest at heart, and there was genuine cause for concern.

"How about my dad? Do you know him?"

"Only because I was an ER nurse at Cedar Hills Hospital before I came here. The general consensus is that your dad can do no wrong. He's very dedicated to his patients."

"He is, isn't he? Poor Trey—as James Thomas Brennan III, he's had a lot to live up to."

That could be part of Trey's problem, but it had to be more than that.

"Do you know my cousin Collin?"

He nodded, smiling. "He's engaged to a nurse friend from Cedar Hills."

"I'm supposed to be a bridesmaid at their wedding, but I haven't met the bride yet."

"You'll like Glenda. She's great."

"Collin's not much like his dad, you know," she said cautiously.

So she knew about her uncle Charlie's flirtations. It couldn't be easy for her, coming back to L.A. where so many people thought they knew her because they knew her family.

"Which is Mona's desk?" she asked, leading the way to the front office and picking up the flowers. "In the interest of a peaceful transition, I brought these for her."

The flowers were arranged in a container shaped like a dove. Noah smiled as he pointed out Mona's desk. It looked as if the doc had done her homework and knew what she might expect from Mona.

"And I have this for Vanessa…"

It was a candy dish, shaped like a pair of kangaroos, their pouches full of candy. Beth placed it on the front desk. Vanessa did have a sweet tooth. How had Beth known that? Since she was batting two for two and there were a couple of gift bags remaining, he wondered what she might have for him.

"And for Noah…" The big bag held a long white box, the kind that long-stemmed roses came in.

Roses? For him?

But the "flowers" were big chocolate chip cookies attached to long green wires sprouting leaves. "Have you ever had a cookie bouquet?" she asked.

"No, this is a first," he said, pleased with his gift. "My daughter's going to love these."

"I saw her picture on your desk when I was moving in. I thought she would like these even if you're not a cookie kind of guy."

Now, that was the way to his heart. A kindness to his little girl topped anything Beth could have given him. "Chocolate chip cookies are her favorite, but she'll think these are too pretty to eat."

"I know!" Beth said with that soft laugh he was getting to know. "That's why I got these." She handed over the smaller bag which held a commercial brand of chocolate cookies with icing. "These are for eating until the novelty of the others wears off."

Three for three. She couldn't do better than that. "I have something for you, too," he said, unrolling his daughter's sign.

"Oh, Noah!" Her voice rose in delight.

For a second, he thought his new boss might cry.

"Your daughter made this, didn't she? And she signed her name, Kendra McKnight. We need to put this up for everyone to see."

He couldn't have asked for a better reaction. "I wanted to have it up before you got here."

"Her drawing really looks like the clinic. How old is your daughter?"

"She just turned seven."

"So, she just started second grade?"

He nodded. "She loves school."

"It's very advanced artwork for a child so young," she said with that truly knockout smile, taking the picture to the bulletin board and placing it in the center.

A piercing screech came from the lobby. Noah took a deep breath and geared up for the storm. Hurricane Mona had arrived, and there was no telling the damage she'd do.

Chapter Three

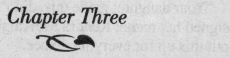

Beth squared her shoulders and prepared for the blast of anger about to walk through the door. As Grandpa had said, getting along with Mona Fitz would be as challenging as getting along with Beth's own mother, but Beth could walk on egg-shells in her sleep.

"Beth Brennan, you've turned this place into a zoo."

"Good morning, Mona," Beth said, as pleasantly as rushing adrenaline would allow. Her body might react to Mona's wild accusations, but her mind would stay clear.

Judging from Mona's flushed face, Beth would say the woman's blood pressure was stroke-high. She'd hate for her first patient to be her own nurse.

"Good morning, Mona," Noah echoed, going to his desk as if this were just another day.

"I suppose you think this is just fine and dandy," Mona said as she brushed by him to her own desk.

"Take another look," he teased. "Notice the pairs? It's Noah's ark."

"Ark, smark," Mona said, her face puckered angrily. "It's not appropriate for a professional office."

"I like it," Noah said, the corner of his mouth lifted in a smile. "But then I get to play the part of Noah. Be nice, and you can be Mrs. Noah—either my wife or my mom."

Beth couldn't believe it. A smile crept over the woman's lips. Grandpa'd said he thought Mona might have a soft spot for Noah. If she did, who could blame her? Noah seemed to be as nice as he was good-looking. Even better, he didn't seem to know it.

If he'd been this nice when they met, why couldn't she remember him? Guys this great weren't forgettable.

Mona shoved her purse into the bottom drawer of her desk and noticed her flowers.

Beth was counting on those flowers. What woman could resist something that lovely, to say nothing of the sweet dove container?

"Achoo!" Mona sneezed, not once but again. Grabbing a tissue, she held it to her nose. "Noah, get those flowers out of here." Another sneeze punctuated her complaint.

Beth bit her lip, trying not to laugh. A child could have faked sneezes better than that.

"Your office?" Noah muttered, barely suppressing a grin as he walked by her with the flowers.

She nodded. Perfect. It would keep Mona out.

"All better?" she asked as Mona's sneezing ended miraculously. "Are you taking something for that allergy, or can I prescribe something?"

"No, you can not!" Mona pointedly ignored Beth.

"Oh, wow!" Someone in the lobby liked the ark.

Beth opened the door and saw a beautiful dark-haired young woman with absolute delight in her sparkling eyes.

"Would you look at the aquarium! And all the little fish! And the darling animal chairs for the kids! This is unbelievable! Hey, Noah! You have an ark out here!"

Noah joined her, wearing a big matching grin. "Kendi's going to love this, isn't she, Vanessa?"

"Oh, she will. All the kids will!"

The glowing approval was a boost after Mona's reaction.

"Hi, Dr. Brennan. I'm Vanessa Taylor, as you've probably figured out, and I'm so happy you're here."

How nice that her patients' first impression would be this lovely young woman's smile. "Hi, Vanessa. Please call me Beth."

"Really?" Vanessa looked as if she'd been offered a raise. "But what if I forget around the patients? Maybe I should call you Dr. B or something?"

"Pfft!" The sound was comically incongruous coming from an impeccably groomed woman. Mona's manicured nails matched the rose color on her thin lips and the flowers of her smock. There wasn't a hint of gray in her upswept black hair, and her pants, shirt and shoes were very white.

"A man of Dr. Crabtree's stature didn't require a nickname," she said with a sniff.

But the Brennan kids had given him one anyway. *Dr. Crabby* had seemed perfect back then. When Beth knew him as an adult and realized he was just shy, she'd felt bad about that.

"Let's go with *Beth* or *Dr. Beth,*" she told Vanessa.

"Got it!" Vanessa said, heading for her desk. She spotted the kangaroo candy dish and stopped. "Look at this! It is *so* cute. Thank you, Dr. Beth."

Beth nodded, feeling exceptionally good about how things were going. "Let's all get settled, then we'll take a little tour and go over a couple of new procedures."

Mona swung around. "A *tour?*" Her shrill

voice could have stripped paint from a wall. "I hardly need a tour! I was here in this office, taking your temperature, before you knew how to count, Beth Brennan."

"You were, weren't you?" Beth struggled to be cordial when every instinct said her grandfather was right and Mona Fitz should go.

"Dr. Crabtree took good care of all you little Brennans, though a lot of thanks it got him."

Beth wasn't sure what that meant, but, trying again to be nice, she said, "It must seem strange that most of us are doctors here now."

"It isn't strange at all! Or it wasn't until today. Your brother and your cousin know how to fit in. They haven't created an eyesore like that mess outside."

This disrespect had to end. No one should have to work in unpleasant conditions. "Mona, do our patients and their parents still call you by your first name?"

"Of course! My name hasn't changed."

"With respect for your many years on the job, I think it's time you were called Ms. Fitz."

Clearly, Vanessa and Noah hadn't heard Mona called that or thought how the two syllables sounded together. To their credit, neither cracked a smile, though Vanessa rushed to the restroom and Noah checked on a lab report.

"My name is Mona!" the woman said, her voice quivering with rage.

"Are you sure?" Beth said doubtfully. "It's important to treat everyone with respect, don't you think?"

Whew! If looks could kill, she'd be dead. Mona's glare was so piercing that Beth had the urge to check for entry wounds, but Mona turned abruptly to her desk.

Beth took a deep breath and walked down the hall to her office, almost skipping. That had gone better than she'd expected, even though she had prayed it would. There was nothing that the Lord and she couldn't handle.

Grandpa'd said there was no way she could handle Mona. Ha! Nothing fired Beth's determination like being told what she couldn't do. They would get along fine.

Beth opened the door to her office and paused to see if it still felt as if she were trespassing there. Missing were Keith's books, personal items and diplomas, but everything else was as he'd left it, everything but the flowers she'd intended for Mona.

Noah had placed them on the massive mahogany desk. Beth leaned down and sniffed their lovely fragrance. What a shame that Mona couldn't have enjoyed them as a sweet reminder of all that was good and pleasant in this world.

Sitting in Keith's big office chair, Beth swiveled slowly, taking in the view of the clinic's lush grounds, the empty bookshelves, the armchairs in front of her desk, the monstrous mahogany desk and the credenza behind her. She would feel more at home when her diplomas were on the wall and the furnishings were her own. There'd been so much to do, her office had been her last priority.

Lord, thank you for what I have, and help me do this job right. I don't want to let Grandpa down.

"Dr. Beth." Noah stood at the open door, holding two more floral arrangements. "Where would you like these?"

The flowers were extraordinary, but the guy holding them took her breath away. It wasn't as if she hadn't seen her share of good-looking men, but something about Noah McKnight stirred her senses. She gestured toward the credenza behind her. "How about there?"

"Looks like a good spot."

She watched him, impressed with the easy way he moved and the conscientiousness with which he placed the flowers, turning them to show them off to best advantage. Some guys would have plunked them down any which way. Either he had an artistic flair or he liked things done right.

"Is that okay?" He gestured toward the flowers.

"It's perfect, but…"

"What?" Instant concern covered his face.

The look on his face seemed so familiar. She had to have seen it before. "I just wondered if you could drop the formality and just call me Beth."

"The first name is important to you, isn't it?" he said with a quick smile that deepened faint laugh lines around his eyes.

He hadn't always been the serious guy Keith Crabtree had described. "I do like first names," she said. "They seem more…friendly."

"And you want to be friends?" he said, his eyes narrowed as if he didn't quite believe it.

"Well, sure. And a friend would sit down for a minute." She tapped her desktop. "Keith had our morning patients rescheduled. We aren't seeing anyone until after lunch."

He sat on the edge of her desktop, balancing himself with one hand, not crowding her space, but close enough that she noticed his tanned muscular arm. And the rest of him, too. Blue scrubs had never looked better on anybody, and she'd seen a lot of blue scrubs.

"Not all doctors are friendly with staff," he said.

She couldn't argue that. The older generation of physicians had their hierarchy of propriety, which some of her peer group still valued, but not her. "I think of us as a team—you, Mona, Vanessa and me."

"Mona? Not Ms. Fitz?"

She bent her head, not wanting him to see her pleasure in winning one tiny battle. "She's Mona…for now."

"For the record," he said, "that's the first time I've seen anyone shut Mona down."

"Really? I'm not usually known for my great assertiveness, but you've been around doctors. You know how we can pull out the sharp comment to get what we want, stat."

He laughed, showing off those laugh lines again. "You just showed who was the boss. Mona's not used to that."

"I don't really want to be 'the boss.' Like I said, we're a team, and we'll find a way to get along. Mona's a fixture here, and she's a first-rate nurse, or Keith Crabtree wouldn't have kept her on all these years."

Noah's eyes drifted, exactly as a person's might if he knew something more than he planned to share.

"Noah?" She wouldn't let him get away with that. "What aren't you telling me?"

He spoke slowly, as if he were choosing his words carefully. "Keith Crabtree was a very private person. I worked with him for two years and didn't know what he did in his spare time…other than fish. I didn't know what his wife was like, how long they'd been married before she died or anything about their baby."

"What baby?"

"Exactly. On the credenza behind you, there was a picture of a baby who died from SIDS. I caught Mona holding the picture once, and I could tell the child was special to her—maybe because she was the baby's godmother, or because she felt so bad for Keith. They worked together a long time."

"I just knew Keith as my pediatrician and Mona as his nurse," Beth said. "I don't remember that he, his wife or Mona ever came to our family's New Year's Eve parties, though I'm sure they were invited. Everyone at the clinic is. I missed the party last year, being in New York, but I was there the year before. I don't remember seeing you. Did I miss meeting you then?"

"I wasn't there."

"Not a party person?"

"My wife was the party person, not me," he said quietly. "She died the preceding October."

"I'm so sorry."

"It's okay. That was two years ago. My daughter and I are doing fine." But his eyes said he remembered the pain.

She'd seen him look that way.

It all came back to her—things she remembered and the one thing she hadn't. "I just remembered when we met."

He looked at her, his eyes as intense as they'd been that terrible day.

"Isn't the mind amazing? I remembered how proud Grandpa was, introducing me as the seventh Brennan to join the clinic. I've relived Mom's mental meltdown many, many times. But I forgot you."

"That's understandable," he said solemnly.

"But I felt so grateful when you came to my rescue. I was too upset to tell you that or what a comfort you were."

"You had a lot going on that day."

"The worst day of my life." Tears weren't far away. They hadn't been that day either.

"Are you okay?" he asked, as he had that day.

She remembered. It was in the hallway after Grandpa told her he didn't want her around for a while. "You asked the same thing then."

"And you said you were, but I knew you weren't."

"You could tell?"

He nodded, a rueful smile on his lips. "For months after Merrilee died, I told people I was okay when I wasn't. Sometimes we can't talk about what hurts."

"Does it still hurt, Noah?"

"Well, I'm talking about it, so it must be better," he said with a smile that lifted one corner of his mouth. "When Kendi seemed to miss her mother less, that helped me."

"Does your family help with your daughter?"

"Neither Merrilee or I had family."

"None?"

Noah dreaded the full-blown sympathy that was sure to come if Beth asked many questions about his background. He would try the short version first and hope it would be enough for today.

"No family," he confirmed. "It's just my daughter and me. Kendi's babysitter, Harlene, lives next door, and she's like family."

For a second, Beth studied him as if she were trying to diagnose a major disease. She was an intelligent woman or she wouldn't have an M.D. As any bright person would, she would figure the odds of both of Kendi's parents having no family and wonder about it.

"Noah…"

Here it came. A question he wouldn't want to answer.

"Would you care to adopt Trey?"

He laughed, just a little, then a lot. The unexpected offer, delivered so seriously, was great.

He was going to love working with Beth. "Thanks, but no thanks."

"Let me know if you change your mind. But if you take him, you've got to keep him."

What a cool sense of humor. He was still smiling. "Who are your flowers from?"

She took the card from the vase of orchids and palm foliage. "This one is from my brother Ry."

She handed the card to him and he read out loud, "'Be strong. Be courageous. Don't be afraid of them for the Lord your God will be with you.' Afraid of who? The patients…or Mona?"

She grinned and gave him a thumbs-up. "Mona did scare all of us kids, but Ry's scripture probably includes the BMC staff. I've known a lot of these people since I was a kid, and I've even babysat for some of their kids. Don't be surprised if you hear somebody call me Bethie."

"Will you mind?"

"Not unless it's Mona."

That made him smile. He was already having more fun than he'd ever had working for Keith.

He watched her read the card from the arrangement of yellow roses. It must have been more sentimental because she dabbed a tear from her eye.

"This one is from Ry's wife. Meg was my best friend all the years we were growing up. Her family was closer to Ry and me than our own. The people we choose to love often mean more to us than the family we're born into, especially the people who share our faith."

So, Beth Brennan was a religious person. That would make Vanessa happy. She went to church all the time.

"I've only been a Christian a couple of years, but I know there's power in prayer," she said with conviction.

Faith? Prayer? This would be a good time to go back up front. He slid off the desk.

"Noah, do you believe in prayer?"

He'd stayed too long.

"You don't have to answer that," she said quickly. "I shouldn't have asked, not in a place of business."

"No, it's okay." It wasn't in him to discourage another's faith, even if he no longer shared it.

"I'm praying for a way to be friends with Mona."

"Knee pads," he said without thinking.

"What?" She looked startled.

"You're gonna need 'em if you're praying for that."

The corners of Beth's mouth tilted upward in the cutest smile. "You're probably right. It could take a while."

He hadn't noticed that particular smile before. The patients were going to love that smile.

She opened her closet and retrieved one of several crisp white lab coats embroidered with Beth Brennan, M.D. Slipping into one, she hooked her stethoscope around her neck and eyed the flowers from her brother and his wife.

"I hate to leave all these beautiful flowers back here. What do you think? Should we share these with our patients in the lobby? Or would Mona's allergy flare up?"

"There's a big vase of red roses there now, and they're not bothering Mona at all."

"Let me guess. They're from my grandfather."

He nodded, grinning at her quick assessment. "I believe the card did say that. Mona read the card and put the flowers on the counter for everyone to see."

"Good for her."

That comment knocked him out. As hateful as Mona had been, it said a lot that Beth wasn't nursing a grudge. She was better than he was, to move on that fast. The gossips around here were going to be so disappointed, with nothing to complain about Beth.

"Bad news," Mona said as Beth and Noah reached the front office. "Our computers are down."

Vanessa looked worried. "I'm sorry, Dr. Beth. I've called technical support, but they can't get here until this afternoon."

"I'm sure we'll survive," Beth said. Her laptop was loaded with data they needed for the day.

"Why don't you call your grandfather," Mona said. "He could pull rank and get tech support here quicker."

If that were true—and it might be—didn't Mona realize that one call could leave her unemployed? The only thing saving Mona's job was Beth and her need to show God's love.

"Not having the computers won't be a big inconvenience this morning," she said pleasantly. "We won't be seeing patients right away."

Mona snorted. "Your first patient is scheduled minutes from now. This office sees patients from nine to five, and it's almost nine. Too bad we won't have time for your little *tour,* Dr. Beth."

Beth looked at Noah to check his reaction. His arms were folded, and his steady gaze asked if he should jump in and set Mona straight.

That he waited, instead of doing it, made Beth like him even more. "Actually, Mona, it was Dr. Crabtree's suggestion that we take time for staff orientation. Our morning patients have been rescheduled. He was wonderfully cooperative in the transition."

Mona sniffed, somewhat mollified. "Dr. Crabtree *is* the consummate professional."

"He certainly is," Beth agreed, going for a conciliatory tone. "Now, let's begin by going over the procedures we'll use as a team."

Noah wheeled his office chair around to face her and whipped out a notepad and pen. Vanessa also prepared to take notes. Mona drummed her nails on her desk and glanced nervously at the lobby window as if a patient might show up and catch them unprepared.

"When I talked to Dr. Crabtree," Beth began, "he was very happy with the way you three worked together. I see no need to change the procedures you're familiar with. If we need to make adjustments along the way, we will. For now, I'll do most of the adjusting."

Mona looked surprised. She stared at Beth as if she had to replay the words to make sure she'd heard right.

"Vanessa, in addition to your regular tasks, I want you to take pictures of each patient." Beth pulled a camera from her pocket and handed it to the young woman.

"I have one almost like this! I love to take pictures. This will be so cool, Dr. Beth! Do the pictures go in the patients' folders or up on a wall?"

"The folders. It will help all of us put a face to the name if we need to later."

"How do you want to handle call-ins during

office hours?" Mona asked, as if she hoped to put Beth on the spot.

It might be Beth's first day at BMC, but she'd grown up with her family talking shop. She knew her job here.

"It depends," she answered, adopting the no-nonsense manner she used when treating seriously ill patients. Maybe that would put Mona at ease. "If Vanessa takes the call, and it's about more than scheduling, she turns the phone over to you or Noah. The two of you will determine whether I need to get on the phone, return the call or head for the hospital."

"In other words, just the way we did with Dr. Crabtree," Noah said dryly.

"How are you going to handle your after-hours' calls?" Mona asked, ignoring him, but again as if she hoped to catch Beth off guard.

"You three can call me anytime." She handed them a card, listing her phone numbers. "For the patients, again, it depends on the situation. The service will refer some calls to my group, and page me on others."

"Wow, that's just the way Dr. Crabtree did it, too," Vanessa teased.

"We still should verify the procedures," Mona said defensively.

"Yes, we should," Beth agreed, partly because

it was true, but also in an effort to get on Mona's good side, if there was one. "If we're all on the same page, our patients can receive the highest standard of care."

"Once they get past the lobby," Mona sniped.

Enough was enough. *Lord, help me get this right.*

"Mona, you don't like the lobby. We've heard that, and we don't need to hear it again. The lobby stays like it is. Let's move on."

Mona's nostrils flared, and she looked about as angry as a person could be, but she seemed to get the message and didn't respond.

Good. That had gone well. "Now, are we ready for our tour?"

Chapter Four

When Beth opened the door to Exam Room One, the group's reaction was as expected. Vanessa just adored the monkeys. Mona was just appalled. Noah folded his arms and seemed to enjoy the show.

After they'd visited Rooms Two and Three, Vanessa couldn't stop smiling, Mona's mouth had that now-familiar lemon-sucking pucker and Noah leaned against the examining table, looking great in his blue scrubs.

Worried and disapproving, Mona said, "Some of our patients are very ill, Beth. How do you expect to handle them in this environment?"

"It doesn't hurt a child to smile." Beth wondered when Mona had last attended a continuing-education class. "Laughter is good for everyone. Our patients are kids, even the older ones. The sicker they are, the more they need a pleasant distraction." To drive home her point, she opened the hat cabinet.

Mona gasped, and Vanessa laughed out loud.

"Try one on," Beth said, modeling her red satin beret topped with the coiled-wire toy. Vanessa reached for the feathered tiara. Noah chose a cowboy hat with a miniature horse on top.

Mona looked at them as if they'd lost their minds. "I am not wearing anything that ridiculous," she said firmly, glaring at the hats as if they were snakes.

"This may be your one and only chance," Beth teased. "The hats are for me to wear, not you... well, unless it's your birthday or you've brought treats for the office."

Mona threw up her hands. "The parents will think you're ridiculous, Beth Brennan!"

"Well, let's hope so!" Beth had occasionally worn her silly hats around patients since her residency and never encountered anyone who thought they kept her from doing her job. "Playing the clown isn't for everyone, Mona, but I like it. Well, I do as long as I don't have to wear one of those round red noses. They're just not comfortable."

Noah and Vanessa laughed as she intended, but Mona rolled her eyes and turned to leave.

Vanessa stopped her. "Mona, take a picture of us."

"I don't know how."

"It's easy. You can do it." Vanessa showed her and positioned Beth and herself on either side of Noah.

Posing for the picture, Beth's smile came easily. This was a beginning. Antiseptic, impersonal care was out and gentle, loving fun was in.

"I don't know if I did it right," Mona complained, shoving the camera back at Vanessa. "Taking pictures is not my job." She fairly flew out of the room.

"Well, it is *my* job," Vanessa said, "and I need the practice. Let me get a picture of the two of you."

Standing this close to Noah, Beth caught the faint scent of his soap or aftershave, a fragrance she liked very much. She looked up at him and realized he was looking at her as if he really liked what he saw.

Maybe it was the hat.

"Got it," Vanessa said, taking the picture. "That was great! Now one more. Dr. Beth, you pretend to be the doctor."

"'Pretend?'" Beth teased.

Giggling, Vanessa said, "You *be* the doctor and, Noah, you be the patient. Dr. Beth, listen to Noah's heart with your stethoscope. That will make a cute picture."

"I vote for a tongue depressor," Noah said, grabbing one from a jar on the counter behind him. "Doctor Beth can check my tonsils." He wasn't about to let her listen to his racing heart. Standing there beside her, he'd felt like a kid with a crush on the pretty girl at school.

Vanessa agreed and moved them into the pose she wanted.

Noah went along, opening his mouth wide and saying Ah. Could he have felt any sillier?

"Good job," Beth said, completing her exam, giving him one of her knockout smiles and a pat on his shoulder, as if he were one of her patients.

But he liked that pat and wouldn't have minded another. The cowboy hat must have rolled back the years.

"On your way out, cowboy, you can choose between a sticker or a lollipop," Beth said.

"Stickers? Oh, that's new!" Vanessa exclaimed. "We haven't had anything but the lollipops before."

Noah smiled at her enthusiasm and wondered if the combined goodwill of the three of them could help Mona with her outlook on life.

"You know," Vanessa said, looking at the pictures on the digital camera, "you two look great together. Are you seeing anyone, Dr. Beth? Noah isn't."

"Vanessa!" both of them said as a duet.

"Okay, okay! It was just a suggestion." She grinned, shelved her tiara and scooted out of the room.

Noah put his hat away. Beth put hers away. Talk about an awkward moment.

Doctor-nurse romances were as old as medicine itself, but Noah had never been part of that and wouldn't be now, despite this edgy anticipation he felt around Beth. Had he ever felt this aware of Merrilee when they'd first met? Had he noticed things like how pretty Merrilee's smile was or that her eyes were the shade of dark honey?

Blue! Merrilee's eyes were blue. He waited for guilt to punch him in the gut, but he only felt guilty that it didn't. "Vanessa kids around a lot," he said to reassure Beth that he hadn't taken their young receptionist seriously.

Beth nodded and spoke with her crisp professional tone. "We might as well acknowledge that two single people working in the same office are going to be teased until people realize we're just friends."

He was surprised she had the guts to say it, but it was true. People had been trying to set him up almost from the day Merrilee died. Beth Brennan was the hot topic of gossip right now, and he would be mentioned in the same breath that she was…for a while.

"Even if we ignore it, they probably won't stop until one of us starts to see someone," Beth said ruefully.

"It'll have to be you," he said dryly. "My daughter is the only woman in my life."

Beth sighed very unprofessionally. "I hate to date."

She looked so genuinely disgusted that a chuckle escaped. Even disgusted, she looked adorable. His new boss would have no trouble finding someone to date.

"Hey!" She frowned at his laughter. "That's going to cost you. Until I find Mr. Right, I might just act as if I don't mind the teasing. What do you think of that?" she challenged, mischief in her eyes.

She didn't mind if they were linked together? If he couldn't laugh at that, he had no sense of humor at all.

Beth walked toward the front desk, wondering if she'd handled that right. Maybe she shouldn't have been so candid about such a sensitive issue. It didn't seem as if Noah had taken the teasing as lightly as she'd pretended to. Maybe that was his way. Grandpa had called him a serious guy.

For herself, it was all smoke screen. She might try to deny she was attracted to him, but her body told the truth. Around Noah, she felt the symptoms of attraction: shortness of breath, clammy palms, butterflies in her stomach, weak knees—all of it.

She hadn't been this attracted to a man since she was an intern. Sometimes the body got way ahead of the mind. Until it registered the right message, a person just had to deal with it.

Had Noah noticed that her hand actually trembled as she held that tongue depressor in his mouth? Maybe he would think it was first-day nerves. Or low blood sugar.

That was it! She grabbed a lollipop from the treat drawer and stuck it in her mouth.

"Hey, I thought I was the one who earned the lollipop," he said, coming up behind her.

She handed him one. "I forgot to eat breakfast," she said inarticulately with the lollipop stuck in her jaw. In truth, she had. Maybe that *was* why her hand had shaken.

"You have a visitor," Mona said primly, nodding toward the lobby.

Beth looked through the window. Her brother Trey stood with his fists on his hips, his long lab coat tucked behind him. He shook his head as he looked at the new lobby decor.

In the best-case scenario, he'd come to take Mona away. The two of them were made for each other, both uptight and easily riled.

"Good morning, Trey," she said, joining him and licking her lollipop with the sophistication of a four-year-old, a move guaranteed to annoy.

"I can't believe this!" Repulsed, he gestured to her terrific new decor.

"Don't be jealous, Trey. I'll redecorate your office when I have time."

"Why didn't you ask Isabel for help?" Trey thought everything he had was better than others, including his wife, who had been an interior decorator before their marriage.

"Actually, I did," Beth reported with glee. "Give your wife some credit, Trey. She was the designer on this job."

Disapproval cleared from his face like mist in the sun.

"Your son already loves it, especially the fishies. Isabel's bringing him in for his shots next week."

"You're not going to be J.T.'s pediatrician."

"I'm not?" Keith Crabtree had been the baby's pediatrician, and J.T. was still on the schedule.

"My son will have the *best* care possible," Trey said, looking down his nose at her and her lollipop.

Did it give Trey some special joy to be as mean as their mother? "And *my* office can't provide the best care?"

"It could when Keith was here."

Her brother might as well have slapped her across the face. Hard. She practically reeled from the blow. But she was tougher than he might think. Pivoting, she headed for the inner office. "Let us know where to send his records," she said over her shoulder.

Noah wasn't normally a snoop, but he watched Beth and her brother through the window to the lobby. Trey Brennan had just delivered a crushing blow to his boss, and Noah didn't like it. Family or not, he was going out there to back her up if nothing else.

But he met her coming through the door. Her eyes were dark with rage.

"What's wrong?" he asked softly so Mona and Vanessa wouldn't hear.

"Nothing," she said, spitting the words. "I'm fine, or I will be."

"How can I help?" It was more of a reflex than a hope she'd let him do anything. Beth seemed like a woman who fought her own battles.

"You could take the knife out of my back. Trey says he's switching his baby to another pediatrician. I'm not good enough for his son."

Noah could only imagine how that would hurt, but he shrugged. "Well, it's not like you're going to use him for neurological consults."

The pinched look on her face dissolved into a grin. "That's right. I'm not."

"If it's any comfort, your brother is not the most popular doctor in the building."

"He's never been popular anywhere!" She shook her head. "Sometimes I wonder how he lives with himself."

"How do you feel about your uncle Al?"

She looked up with wary eyes. "Why?"

"He called. He's on his way."

Behind them, Mona zipped across the office to open the door to the lobby. "Good morning, Dr. Brennan," she said, professional to the core.

Al Brennan ignored her and greeted Beth with a big hug. "Welcome to the club, Bethie. I see you're all ready for the kiddies." He nodded toward the lobby. "Very cute."

"I'm glad you approve. Some people don't." She glanced Mona's way.

Mona had the good sense to busy herself with a file. Noah moved to his desk, knowing the great doctor would ignore him as well.

"Well, I think the look is perfect for a pediatrician's office. Crabtree, the old penny-pincher, wouldn't spend a cent on the place."

Noah glanced at Mona to get her reaction. Her lips disappeared in a thin line of anger.

"Thank you for taking the time to stop by," Beth said, smiling up at her uncle.

"I thought I ought to personally invite you to lunch tomorrow. Now that we're colleagues, you're more than my favorite niece."

"I'm your only niece, Uncle Al."

Vanessa's glance at Noah said she thought their new boss was a hoot. Noah returned the nod, in full agreement. He sure hadn't expected to like Beth so much or so fast.

They went their separate ways for lunch, but when their first patient arrived, they were ready. Vanessa went into action, taking the baby's picture without being prompted. Noah ushered mother and child into Exam Room One. Mona returned a call to the lab. Beth leaned against the front counter, giving Noah a few minutes to do the intake.

Considering the negatives she'd faced, it was amazing how relaxed she felt. Coming home had been the right thing to do. With God's help, this office would be a sanctuary—a place of peace and healing.

Lord, may all who come here be safe in our care.

It was just a little prayer, but it wasn't the length of the prayers that mattered. Constant connection between herself and the Lord, that was what He asked for. That's what she hoped to learn.

She opened the door to Exam One, looking forward to the best part of this job, playing with a healthy baby while she did a routine exam. Noah's eyes met hers, as if he were asking if she was all right.

She was. Definitely. Having a nurse who was this in tune with her was a gift, and the jitters of attraction for her good-looking male nurse would soon wear off.

He handed over the patient folder, and their routine began. She greeted the parent while Noah prepared the baby's shots. He left to see their next patient while Beth scanned the baby's folder, answered an assortment of questions from the first-time mother and had a great time doing the exam. What a sweet baby! She carried him to the front desk before giving him back to his mom.

Vanessa scheduled the little one's next visit. Mona was still talking on the phone, and Noah was missing, probably with the next patient in Exam Room Two. Everyone seemed to be on familiar ground.

"Dr. Beth, line two," Vanessa said. "It's your dad."

Beth glanced at her watch and started toward her office. She had time to take the call there. As seldom as she talked to her father, she would like the privacy. Maybe he was calling to invite her to dinner. They were both alone, now that her mother was with Aunt Jackie in Tahoe.

"Hi, Dad!" she said, wondering if he remembered his first day here so long ago.

"Beth, I called to say thank-you."

"You're welcome, but for what?" She was the one who should be thanking him for the call.

"I know the pressure you're under, and I know you're at the clinic because Dad wants you there. That was very good of you, Beth."

The words were as unexpected as the way his quiet voice pulled on her heartstrings. Her dad was BMC's star, a thoracic surgeon who put his patients first, but he'd made time for her today. That was a big deal.

"Grandpa's gone out of his way to make things easy for me," she said, putting a smile in her voice, as always, trying to be so charming that her dad wouldn't rush off. "I think it's going to be—"

"Beth, I've got to go. I just wanted to say your mother and I are very proud of you." With that, he disconnected so quickly that neither of them said goodbye.

She glanced at her watch again. The call lasted ten seconds. At most. He hadn't mentioned when she might see him. She hadn't gotten to ask how her mother was doing—if he knew. The call was over so quickly, it had hardly begun. Why had he even bothered to call?

Her heart was heavy as she walked up front. There was a beautiful peace lily with a witty note from her cousin Collin, the anesthesiologist. It made her smile, but she couldn't shake off the disappointment from her dad's call.

Noah said, "The little guy in Two is ready for you."

As soothing as warm butterscotch, Noah's deep voice settled her uneasy spirit, and she felt…better. Just like that. She looked up at him, wondering if he knew.

His eyes lingered on hers as if he might.

"Dr. Beth," Vanessa said anxiously, "your uncle, Dr. Charles Brennan, is in the lobby."

One look through the window to the lobby explained the panic in Vanessa's voice. Her womanizing uncle was flirting with the attractive mother of one of her patients.

Beth hated to have a patient wait while she visited with a family member, but she hustled to the lobby as fast as she could.

"Hey, little Beth!" her uncle said. "I love what you've done to the place."

"Thank you," she said, taking his arm and walking him away from her lobby. "It was sweet of you to stop by, Uncle Charlie."

He leaned down and said softly, "Dad ordered us to roll out the red carpet."

That could explain why her dad bothered to call.

"This business with Mona bad-mouthing the whole family just won't do. Since she's made no secret that she blames us for Keith leaving, it's a good idea for her to know we're all behind you. Beth, why won't you let Dad give her the boot?"

She wished they weren't taking Mona so seriously. "I've become a praying person, uncle. I think this will pass, and we'll get along. And I don't want the talk around here to be that Grandpa's precious granddaughter cost a loyal employee her job."

"Beth, listen to your old uncle Charlie. Life's too short to put up with a bad-tempered woman."

Maybe that was why her uncle was on his fourth marriage.

"How is it going with Mona today?" he asked.

Since there was a good possibility that whatever she told her talkative uncle Charlie would filter to the grapevine, why not give him a report to repeat?

With a robot's mechanical phrasing, she said, "Every-one has been won-der-ful to me. I look for-ward to a long re-la-tion-ship with my staff."

"What?" he asked, chuckling. "Give it to me again."

She repeated the statement the same way.

"I take it this is your official statement."

"That you might want to share with...everyone."

He burst out laughing. "It wouldn't hurt, would it?"

"Probably not."

Sobering, he said, "You know, there was always something fishy going on between Mona and Keith. Dad called her the day after Keith revealed his retirement and offered her an attractive retirement package. The way she complains all the time, he thought she'd jump at the chance to get out of here, but she turned Dad down flat. That makes me nervous. If you insist on keeping her, at least watch your back, Beth."

"Isn't that a little dramatic?"

"Maybe. But I'm glad that you have Noah. He's a good man. He'll look out for you."

"So is Noah my nurse or my bodyguard?" she teased.

"Whatever you want, sweetheart. Whatever you want."

Unfortunately, that was a blank check Beth couldn't afford to cash.

Mona felt as if she were going to explode. Beth Brennan's first day had been a disaster, with the

Brennan clan and a number of other senior BMC staff traipsing in and out all day.

Mona knew who was behind it all. Beth's grandfather, that's who! The old coot.

The final straw was having him arrive moments ago, just as the last patient left. This family and their big show of unity!

She watched the old man shuffle up and down the hall, leaning heavily on his cane, putting his stamp of approval on everything from Beth's ridiculous zoo to her ridiculous hats. Little Bethie was the old man's pride and joy, that was for sure. And she acted as if he were the treasure of her life. It made Mona want to heave.

Clearly, if there was any hope of getting Keith back in the office where they could be together, it was up to her. She would not stand idly by. Neither could she endure this horrible ache of never seeing him, of never hearing his voice. Keith was her rock, the very cornerstone of her existence.

For his sake and for hers, Beth Brennan had to go.

Chapter Five

Noah couldn't remember when he'd driven home on the freeway during rush hour with a smile on his face. He rubbed his hand over his cheeks, not minding one bit that his smiling muscles felt overworked or that this might become a chronic condition.

His new boss had a lighthearted attitude that made a person forget how tough life could be. Every time her mouth tilted up at the corners for that one particular smile, he couldn't help but smile himself.

He needn't have worried about Beth knowing her stuff. She obviously had good training and knew what she was doing. He loved the way she handled the patients and their parents. She hadn't talked down to any of them, and she'd gone out of her way to make them feel safe in her care.

Admittedly, he'd assumed she got the job at BMC because of family connections, but today he'd seen why the chief placed such confidence in his granddaughter.

The only problem with working with her was going to be space, or the lack of it. Doctors' offices were clusters of small spaces. There was the front office, the exam rooms, the storage room—none of which needed to be very large, but when he was with Beth, and that was about half of the time, she was never more than a few feet away.

When Vanessa had taken those pictures of them, Beth was so close he could feel her breath on his face. Then he'd realized she could probably feel his. If that wouldn't make a guy self-conscious, what would? He'd worked with female docs before, but he'd never wondered if he needed a breath mint.

The next freeway exit led to Loma Verde, the little community he'd called home since he'd gotten his first job in the Cedar Hills Hospital ER. Taking the exit, he switched into daddy mode as he did every workday. From now until tomorrow morning, when he would walk Kendi to the babysitter next door, his life would be all about her, though she wasn't supposed to realize that.

As important as it was that Kendi not feel neglected, unloved or in want, it was just as important that she not feel smothered or burdened by being the one person he loved. People who had families took them for granted, but he and Merrilee had never done that. They'd been too long without love not to appreciate what they had.

He turned into their neighborhood and thought that he and Merrilee had chosen a good place for Kendi to grow up. Each small ranch-style house had started with the same floor plan and the same exterior thirty years ago, but families had made them their own with different treatments for their front doors or shutters at the windows. His neighbors were working people who took pride in keeping their homes looking nice.

His house had come with a driveway, a carport and green shutters, which Merrilee had promptly changed to pink. She'd grown pink flowers, too, at the front door and around back, by their little patio. The yard was small and the grass was sparse, as dry as it was in Los Angeles. People in this neighborhood didn't spend their money on sprinkler systems and fancy lawns.

When Merrilee was gone, he and Kendi had missed her so much they could barely make it through the day, but they'd finally developed their own routine. When he pulled into their driveway,

Kendi would be standing in the window of Harlene's house next door, watching for him. As soon as she spotted him, she would pop out of the front door, but wait until his car door opened. When he stepped out of his car, and she knew for sure it was him, his beautiful little girl would fly across the yard and jump into his arms.

That was the best part of his day.

He turned onto his street, and there she was, his little girl, waiting at the window. He got out of the car, and she came running, her long blond hair streaming and her yellow dress fluttering against tanned little legs.

"Dad-dy!" she cried, her sweet face as happy as if he'd been gone for months.

He swept her up in his arms and twirled her around, loving the sound of her delighted giggle. "How's my girl?"

"Tee-riff-ic!" That was his Kendi. She saw the sunny side of life just like her mother had.

"Did you and Harlene have fun today?"

"Can I tell you a secret?" she asked, bending her forehead to his. "Harlene didn't want to go to the park today. She's supposed to take a walk every day, but she didn't, Daddy."

His daughter had a little problem, thinking she was the boss of the world. Rules were her thing. She made it a point to play by them, and when someone else didn't, his baby turned tattletale. They were working on that.

"Harlene said it was too hot to walk, but I don't think so. Do you?"

"It probably felt too hot to Harlene. She doesn't have a cool yellow sundress like you." He planted a kiss on Kendi's neck, so happy to see her that he couldn't bring himself to teach manners just now. "Remember that Harlene doesn't feel good sometimes."

"But I reminded her to take her med'cine."

"Good for you." If allowed, his seven-year-old could probably have given the diabetic woman her insulin injections. Kendi knew what Harlene was supposed to eat and *not* eat, what the numbers meant when Harlene did a finger-prick test and how to call 911 in an emergency. Harlene said she ought to be paying Noah the babysitter money instead of taking it.

"Daddy, it was bor-ing, watching Harlene's TV shows."

"Did you do your homework?"

She cocked her head to one side and gave him a reproving look. "I al-ways do my homework."

"That was a dumb question, wasn't it?"

"You aren't supposed to say *dumb*."

She had him on that one.

"It can make people upset if you say *dumb*."

"Since your homework's done, shall we go to the park?"

"Yes!" She beamed at him, such joy in her blue-violet eyes that he was putty in her hands.

"As soon as I change out of my scrubs, okay?"

"I'll help you, Daddy."

That was his girl, ever the helper. It taxed his creative juices, thinking of ways that she could. "I have something for you to carry." He reached into the car and brought out the long box of cookie-flowers.

"Whoa! That's a big box," she said, her eyes big.

He opened the lid for her to see what was inside.

"Ah!" she gasped in delight. "Cookies? Like flowers?"

"Dr. Beth sent these to you."

"She did? Because I made her the sign?"

"Actually, she had this present for you even before she saw your sign."

"Oh!" Kendi was almost speechless with pleased surprise. "I should make her a picture every day."

"But not to get a present every day, right?"

She gave him a reproving look. "No, Dad-dee. Because she likes pictures. Do you think she would like another rainbow?"

Kendi loved to color rainbows. "Do you know what?" he asked. "Dr. Beth had somebody paint a huge rainbow on our office wall."

"Oh! Really?"

"And she had them paint Noah's ark on the wall. We have two elephants, two giraffes, two of everything. There's an aquarium with two orange fish, two blue fish and two yellow fish."

"And you're Noah," Kendi crooned, catching on quickly. "But you need hair on your chin, Daddy."

"You think I should grow a beard?"

She cocked her head to one side, considering. "Would it tickle when you kiss me?"

"Probably. Do you want a cookie?"

"Yes!" Her eyes lit as she reached for one, but her little hand stopped in midair. "They're too pretty to eat, Daddy."

He laughed to himself and retrieved the bag of chocolate cookies. "Dr. Beth thought you might say that, and she sent these for you to eat first."

"Cool! Can I have one now?"

He tore open the bag as an answer. She reached in for one and crunched down on a chocolate bite. A good parent might have waited until after dinner to let her have the treat, but why should a healthy child wait for something so good, at least once in a while?

They entered the house by the kitchen door, and he lifted her to the stool at the counter. She could have scrambled up there herself, but why miss the chance of holding her again and stealing another kiss, one on the ear that made her giggle.

She reached for a second cookie.

"Want some milk with that?" he asked, getting her yellow glass from the cupboard.

She nodded, her mouth full of cookie.

He helped himself to a cookie and poured more milk.

"Did Dr. Beth like my sign, Dad?"

"Yep. She loved it." Kendi had just started calling him "Dad" sometimes. She seemed to think it was big-girl talk, but if he had his way, she would never grow up.

"Did she hang my sign up?"

"Yep. Right in the middle of the bulletin board where everyone could see it."

"Did she see her name on the picture?"

"She did, and she saw yours. She said that Kendra was a cool name." He reached for a second cookie.

She eyed the bag of cookies and looked up at him. Two was usually the limit.

"One more?" he offered.

"Yep." She dug in the bag. "One more and no more."

He wouldn't mind one more himself. Popping one in his mouth, he headed for his bedroom. She knew his routine. As comfortable as scrubs were, he preferred shorts and a T-shirt when he was home. Shutting the door, he made the switch quickly as routine demanded. If he dawdled, she'd be rapping on the door, wanting to come in.

"Dad?" she said with a rap on the door. They had a strict closed-door policy. "I'm ready to help."

He opened the door, and she scanned his length, checked out what he had on and went to his closet, coming back with his running shoes. "You need your shoes, Dad."

They were heavy for her to carry, but it made her happy, being in charge and telling him what to do. "Are you going to change?" he asked, knowing the answer.

"Why?" she asked as if he were crazy.

"Some little girls like to wear shorts or jeans when they go to the park."

"Not me. I L-O-V-E, love dresses!"

So had her mother. And perfume and jewelry and her closet full of shoes. Kendi was just like her except Merrilee had been a brunette. While he put on his sneakers, Kendi twirled at the foot of his bed until she lost her balance and her long hair swirled across her face.

There must have been blondes somewhere in his

gene pool or Merrilee's, but neither of them knew enough about their families to talk about it. He'd spent a lot of time, wondering about his real family, but that had changed when Kendi was born.

Loving her as he did, he couldn't understand his own parents. If they'd chosen not to raise him—or couldn't—why hadn't they signed for him to be adopted by people who would have given him a permanent home?

Beth parked her VW in the Cedar Hills Hospital physicians' lot and made her way to the pediatric wing, a route so familiar she could have managed it with her eyes shut. As a resident, she'd practically lived here, but tonight she only had evening rounds.

In the doctors' lounge, she slipped into a lab coat and looped her stethoscope around her neck. Sitting at the nurses' station was her favorite nurse, a seasoned Christian who'd witnessed to Beth about the Lord many times before her brother Ry had prayed with her.

"Well, look who's back! Couldn't live without us, huh?" Sandy Beecham teased, her dear face full of welcome.

"Just doing rounds," Beth said, claiming a hug. "I'll be in and out before you know it."

"You've already admitted patients?"

"No, it's my turn to see the patients in my group."

"That would be doctors Knedler, Moffitt, Schwabe and Teal?" Sandy asked, reaching for the charts of their patients.

"The very ones." Beth looked through the charts to see what she needed to do.

"Beth!" That voice used to make her heart race.

Dr. Luke Jordahl, her former attending, smiled down at her as if just seeing her made his day. "I knew you'd be back," he said, the lines around his hazel eyes crinkling as he smiled. He gave her shoulders a loving squeeze.

"Well, this is where my patients are," she answered, moving away from his touch, though once she had loved it.

"You have patients here already?" That deep, raspy voice used to send butterflies spiraling in her stomach.

"They're the patients of my peds group."

He looked at the stack of charts. "No problems here."

She didn't doubt his assessment. As her attending, Luke Jordahl had driven her crazy, looking over her shoulder, but she was a better doctor for it. No one had better diagnostic skills than Luke. She'd wondered if she hadn't fallen for him because he was such a good doctor. And liar.

"Have you had dinner?" he asked, his eyes scanning her face as if he couldn't get enough of the sight of her.

She knew better than to believe that, but this was the perfect opportunity to get their relationship started off on a new track. Since they would run into each other often, they needed new boundaries. Her goal was to be friendly, as a Christian should be. Nothing more. For sure, he needed to stop the flirting and realize he couldn't play with her heart again.

"I haven't eaten," she said, "and I'm hungry enough to eat hospital meat loaf and instant mashed potatoes."

"Hold on to these charts, will you, Sandy?" he said, handing them off.

Sandy looked over her glasses at him, then lifted one warning brow at Beth.

Beth nodded. She knew what she was doing.

On the elevator, she talked about her first day at BMC and tried not to mention Noah more often than she did Vanessa and Mona.

Luke was still too handsome for his own good, in a shaggy sort of way, especially compared to Noah's clean-cut good looks. His prematurely gray hair did look great against his tan, though. He had soulful, compassionate eyes that could connect with a child or melt a woman's heart and make her believe she was the only one in the world.

They selected their food in the cafeteria and sat down at a table for two in the physicians' dining area. She wolfed down greasy meat loaf, canned green beans that were barely warm and instant mashed potatoes as if they were good, but she was nervous, thinking about what she wanted to say.

Luke ate a few bites from his matching dinner before pushing it away. "I missed you, Beth," he said, his voice raspy and low, his hazel eyes puppy-dog soft.

Adrenaline charged through her body as if it still mattered what he thought. She blotted her lips with a paper napkin and tried to think of a response that would get their relationship on to the new track.

"You know what I missed, Luke? I missed this meat loaf. Either it's wonderful or I ate it so often while I was a resident that I'm completely addicted. Are you going to eat the rest of yours?" She forced herself to look longingly at his cold food.

A fleeting look of disgust crossed his handsome face, but he pushed his tray over. "There you go. Eat up."

That look of disgust was perfect, a very nice first step. "I really shouldn't," she said, digging into the meat loaf. "Thanks for sharing," she said, wiping grease from her mouth.

"I'd like a chance to share more than a meal with you, Beth," he said. "While you were gone, I realized how badly I messed up when we were together."

The urge to snap off a sarcastic reply was hard to resist. She wished Luke could know what it felt like to love someone dearly, only to discover she wasn't the only one he claimed to love. When she'd realized he couldn't be true to one woman if his life depended on it, she'd moved on, though she hadn't trusted anyone since.

"You'll never know how many times I thought about coming to see you in New York," he said, his eyes roving her face. "I didn't think you'd want to see me."

He'd been right about that.

"When I heard you were back, I let myself hope we could start over. I've changed, Beth," he said earnestly.

Good for him. He needed to change, but not for her.

"I see you don't trust me, but you will. I can wait."

She had to give him credit for sustaining the romantic tone while she ate like a pig. She took a drink of her soda, stalling for time. How could she show him Christ's love, yet quash this proposal of new friendship? Was there any scripture that said she had to give him a chance to let him walk on her heart a second time?

"You know, I have this rule," she said, choosing her words carefully while she played with her straw. "A guy gets to break my heart once. Just once."

The pain on his face seemed genuine. "I was an idiot."

That was something they could agree on.

"Beth, I didn't know what I had with you. I'd never been in love. It scared me. What if we just take it slow," he said, his eyes pleading. "Let me prove how much you mean to me. We were perfect together."

It had felt perfect to her at the time. Later, she'd felt perfectly stupid, letting herself fall for an unfaithful man.

"We made a great team. We can again."

A team?

"I wish you knew how much I love the idea of being with you every day, all the time."

Every day? Literally? This was not a man to talk marriage. What did he have in mind?

Suddenly, she got it. She'd been a little slow, but she definitely understood where Luke was going with this.

"Every day, all the time?" she echoed, putting a bit of wonder in her voice. "Luke, could it be that you're thinking of going into private practice?"

"I might be," he said lovingly, as if he was proud of her for getting on board and seeing the wonderful future that lay before them. "We would make a great team."

She took a deep breath, trying to hold on to her temper. "A great team. I see what you mean. You with your pediatric experience and me with my office at Brennan Medical Clinic. The only problem with that is…"

He leaned forward, concerned and ready to solve that problem.

"I already have a team. I have my two nurses and my receptionist. We worked together like clockwork today. I don't need a partner."

He looked genuinely crushed. She knew the feeling. Getting away from him when she moved to New York had given her a chance to heal.

Either Luke was a first-class actor or her response had actually taken the wind out of his sails. Had he been that sure that she would fall for him again? Was his ego that gigantic, or did he truly care?

Lord, if I've misjudged Luke, let me feel sorry for him or loving or…anything that keeps me from walking away.

She waited.

"Dr. Beth Brennan, please report to pediatrics," the PA announced. It wasn't a voice from heaven exactly, but Beth smiled and glanced heavenward. *Just in case You set that up, Lord, thank you.*

Chapter Six

Noah heard his daughter singing in her bedroom as he slicked the comforter over his bed and added the decorative pillows, tidying the room just the way Merrilee used to. He turned, knowing Kendi would be at his door in a heartbeat, and she was, her eyes as bright as if she'd been up for hours. Even when she was tiny, she'd started her day singing before her feet hit the floor.

"Good morning to my dad-dee," she sang.

"Good morning to my pud-din'," he sang back, his voice early-morning husky and so much lower than hers.

"I'll fix you break-fast," she sang.

"I'll wash your clothes," he returned. If anyone heard their peculiar daddy-daughter operetta, they might question his fitness to parent. It was Merrilee who'd started this ritual with Kendi, but he'd continued it because his baby had so obviously wanted her little life to remain the same.

She waltzed down the hall toward the kitchen, humming away, and he gathered up a load of clothes for the washer. While he started the laundry, Kendi poured cereal from the box he'd put on the kitchen counter last night, along with two cereal bowls. She got the spoons. He poured the milk and juice. She climbed onto the counter stool, and he sat beside her. She took his hand and bowed her head.

"Thank you, God, for this be-yoo-ti-ful day and for our food. Help Daddy be a good nurse to the kids at work and help me be a good nurse at Harlene's and a good friend at school. In Jesus' name, amen!"

Kendi was the official praying person at their house, and that was her standard morning prayer on school days. He wished he had her sweet, simple faith. Belief in God was a great comfort to those who still thought He cared.

She spooned her cereal, as always, just as carefully and tidily as she could, wiping her mouth with a napkin in a style her mother would have been proud of. He followed suit just to keep her from getting on his case about manners.

"Daddy, what color hair does Dr. Beth have?"

Were they back to that? Last night, she'd interrogated him about his new boss until he'd threatened no bedtime story if she didn't quit. "Like I told you last night, blond, like you."

"Blond is yellow, right?"

She knew that. To Kendi, anything yellow was the absolute best.

"Is her hair long?"

"Nope, kind of short."

"Was it curly or straight?"

He had to think. Describing hair was not his forte. "Straight, I guess, or kind of…fluffy?"

"Does she wear glasses?"

"Nope." Where did Kendi get all these questions?

"How old is she?"

He shrugged. If he didn't answer, maybe she would hop to another topic. She usually did.

"Is she as old as you?"

"I don't know."

"Just guess."

Even though Beth had finished college early, so he'd been told, with the years it took to get through med school, residency and her stint in New York, she had to be close to thirty. Since he'd just turned thirty-one, he answered, "Maybe not quite as old as me."

"Does she like to read books?"

"Probably. Doctors have to read a lot of books before they become doctors."

"Does she like kids?"

"She's a pediatrician, and you know that's a doctor for kids, so I'm sure she does."

"Does she say her prayers at night?"

Remembering Beth's talk of faith, he felt confident that she did. "I expect so."

"Can she cook macaroni and cheese?"

Noah stopped eating and looked at his child. That was Kendi's favorite dish—which he made for her all of the time. "If I can cook it, I suppose she can, at least the kind that comes in a box."

"But can she bake, Daddy? I love to bake."

A child Kendi's age wasn't particularly subtle. His daughter was asking if Beth Brennan had mommy potential. "Harlene lets you bake."

"I like to bake at my house. Can Dr. Beth bake?"

"I don't know." It was time Kendi got her mind on something else.

"Do you like her, Dad?"

"She brought cookies for my Kendi, so, sure, I like her. Why don't we eat one of those flower cookies for dessert?"

"Dessert for breakfast?" she asked incredulously.

It was a first, but that's all he could think of to divert her attention. Kendi was always full of questions, but not ones like this. He opened the long box and offered Kendi first choice.

She handled the cookie flower carefully,

nibbling at the edge as if she weren't quite sure she should be. He bit into his, manlike, expecting her to be appalled.

And she was. "Daddy, you only get one flower cookie."

"Just one and no more?"

She grinned, recognizing the phrase she used all the time. But then she pointed her finger at him. "Daddy! You changed the subject!"

He couldn't catch a break.

"When I asked you if you like Dr. Beth, I mean like Richie Hoover likes me. You didn't tell me."

"Like I told you yesterday, a man doesn't 'like' his boss, puddin', not that way."

He could almost see the wheels turning in her mind. Once Kendi got an idea in her head, she seldom let it go.

He supposed he should be grateful that the questions meant Kendi didn't miss Merrilee as much as she used to, but that didn't mean he was ready to find her a new mother. Even if he were, it wouldn't be a woman as far out of his league as Beth Brennan.

Beth sat at Vanessa's desk with a phone to her ear, waiting for a lab report. Vanessa or one of the nurses could have made this call, but she had no patients waiting, and the three of them were busy.

Her stomach growled with hunger, which meant it was nearly time to have lunch with Uncle Al. No doubt he would offer plenty of advice on how she ought to run her office.

But things had gone well this morning. Mona hadn't exactly been friendly, but at least she was civil. Maybe she'd realized her anger was misdirected. It wasn't Beth's fault that Keith had left abruptly without a proper goodbye. In Beth's opinion, Keith had treated his faithful nurse quite shabbily.

With nothing better to do while she waited for the lab report, Beth's eyes roamed the room. Noah sat at his desk, making a call of his own, checking on a patient's aftercare. Some women noticed a man's eyes or his height first thing. For Beth, it was shoulders, and Noah's were perfect. Wide, but not too wide; strong, but not body-builder muscular. She wondered what he did to work out. His well-toned body didn't get that way by itself.

He turned and caught her staring, but she could handle that. She let her eyes drift to the ceiling, the cold-air vent, the drinking fountain. Was he watching?

Sneak peek. Yes, he was.

So, maybe he would look away if she pretended to listen to someone speaking on the phone. She leaned forward, listening intently to nothing, a pen in her hand, ready to take notes. He smiled and turned back to his desk.

She'd just faked a phone conversation! How bad was that?

What was it about this guy? In a heartbeat she'd traded her integrity for a way to get out of trouble, just like a kid. And this morning, when she'd accidentally brushed against him in the hallway, she'd all but come unglued. That couldn't keep happening.

She really should start to see someone…and not just to influence clinic gossip. A woman ought to have some sort of a love life when she was thirty.

In New York City, there had been a zillion people, but eligible bachelors didn't frequent the free clinic where she'd worked or the little store-front church where she'd worshipped. She should have gone out more.

Here in L.A., Noah was the only single guy she'd met, but they had to be out there. She couldn't keep getting all twittering and stupid around her good-looking nurse.

Lord, please, may I meet a man of my own…a man to love, to cherish—

Wedding words! Those were wedding words!

Lord, I'm not exactly desperate, but I am ready to meet the man of Your choice. When You make it

*clear he's my guy, I would like to be married. I
know women—and men, too—make the mistake
of setting the bar too high and miss the partners
You intend. Don't let me miss my guy, Lord.*

A whiff of very pleasant-smelling aftershave
made her open her eyes. Noah stood at the
counter, a patient chart in his hand, watching her.

"Are you still on hold?" he said softly, his voice
a buttery baritone.

It didn't feel like she was on hold. Every cell
in her body perked up with him standing this near.
But she knew he meant the call, and nodded, admitting the truth.

"Maybe I shouldn't mention this," he said hes-
itantly, "but you were watching me, right?"

Oh, for those pre-Christian days when she could
have lied her way out of this. "Um-hmm," she re-
sponded reluctantly, gearing herself up to apologize.

"I don't want you to think that I mind."

What was she missing? Nobody liked being
watched. Was he that vain or totally weird?

"It's cool with me that you're…cautious, Beth.
A good doc ought to observe the work of her staff
before she trusts her patients with them."

Talk about a misdiagnosis! She felt entirely
stupid. "Thank you, Noah," she said, clearing her
throat, switching into professional mode. "I ap-

preciate your attitude and the fact that you told me. I wish I'd been more subtle with the observation, but you're right. And I like what I see."

Were his eyes laughing at her?

"Of your work," she added quickly. "It's first-rate, tip-top, great…really great."

His mouth lifted at one corner in a smile that might be acknowledging her compliment, or, quite possibly, her tendency to babble when nervous. Tip-top? Where had that come from? She should never speak again.

"If you see things you want done differently," he said, "just tell me."

"And if you see things I'm not covering, I want you to tell me."

He put out his hand, ready for a handshake. "Deal?"

"Deal." She slipped her hand into his…and wanted to leave it there. She really was pathetic.

"Your cousin Collin's office called. He has a new neighbor with a sick child, a five-year-old with an earache. That will be your last patient before lunch."

Noah opened the door to the lobby and called, "Matthew Allen Scott?"

Through the receptionist's window Beth saw a willowy redhead in her midthirties stand and take the arm of a sad-faced little boy and guide him to the inner office, though the woman's eyes were on Noah.

"Your eyes are the color of freshly brewed coffee," the woman said to Noah, breathlessly.

Vanessa joined them just in time to hear that. The comical way she glanced at the woman and back to Beth was Beth's undoing. Even suppressed, a giggle escaped, which, unfortunately, sounded like a piggy snort. That tickled Beth even more and set Vanessa off into full-fledged, silent laughter—the worst kind to control. Trying to maintain her dignity, Beth ended up coughing.

Noah rolled his eyes and handed her a wad of tissues.

"Are you okay?" the woman asked solicitously.

"Never better," Beth said, struggling to gain a professional demeanor.

"Would you step up on the scale for me, Matthew?" Noah asked, so gentle that Beth's heart turned over. It got to her every time a man was sweet to a kid.

Listlessly, the child followed Noah's instructions.

"You come very highly recommended, Dr. Brennan," the woman said to Noah, flirting outrageously. "My neighbor, Dr. Collin Brennan, says his cousin is a brilliant pediatrician."

Noah's long-suffering sigh made Beth clasp

her hand over her mouth. She would not laugh again. Vanessa moved out of sight to keep out of trouble.

"He told you that, did he?" Noah said straight-faced.

"Yes, and he says you're single. I am, too, at the moment."

Beth couldn't wait to see how Noah would handle this.

"Collin was right about his cousin being a brilliant pediatrician," he said calmly, "but the doctor is sitting over there." He pointed to Beth. "I'm the nurse."

Beth gave a little wave.

"I thought she was the receptionist," the woman said, appalled at her gaffe.

"No, that would be me," Vanessa said, coming out of hiding.

Beth rose and went to shake the woman's hand. "I borrowed Vanessa's chair while I made a call. I'm sorry for the mix-up, Ms. Scott." She bent down to the child's level and touched his shoulder. "Hi, Matthew. I'm Dr. Beth. Someone told me you have an earache. Is that right?"

He nodded, tears in his eyes.

Poor little guy. She couldn't wait to make him feel better. "Do you like giraffes, Matthew?"

He nodded.

Beth rose and took his hand. "Then, let's go into this exam room. There're some funny giraffes in there. I wonder if giraffes ever have an earache? Do both of your ears hurt or just one?"

He pointed to his right ear.

"Can I take a look and see why it hurts?" She lifted him to the table and began her exam, chatting with him about his kindergarten field trip to the zoo. It made a good topic of conversation. The parent was less likely to answer for the child, and Beth had a better chance to assess his condition.

Actually, she need not have tried so hard. Ms. Scott's focus was solely on Noah as she answered his questions about Matthew's condition and medical history. Noah might not be the doctor, but he *was* single. That apparently made him worthy of Ms. Scott's attention.

But the woman's efforts were in vain. Noah did his job with all the charisma of a rock. Beth hid a smile. So this was the serious side of Noah that she'd heard about.

Matthew needed a round of antibiotics and a huge dose of tender loving care. Beth hoped that Ms. Scott would be a better mom when she was alone with her little boy than she'd been here in the office.

Lord, put lots of people in Matthew's life to love him.

As the child of parents who barely knew they had children, she knew the importance of kind words and loving smiles. Even a child who seemed to have everything could be starving for affirmations that somebody cared.

She gave the little guy a big hug and turned him over to Vanessa for the selection of a sticker and a lollipop. His mother gave Noah one last lingering look.

"That's not going to be the last time that happens," Noah said, following Beth to her office.

"What? A mother describing your eyes perfectly?" Beth teased as she traded her lab coat for a blazer.

His coffee-colored eyes sparked with indignation. "You know what I mean. I'll be mistaken as the doctor."

"And you think I haven't been mistaken as the nurse?"

"You probably have," he said dryly. "Maybe my daughter won't run into gender bias by the time she's grown."

"Your example of working at a job you obviously love ought to help."

That seemed to please him.

"Your height probably contributes toward the stereotyping," she said. "Tall people are generally perceived to be in charge."

He nodded agreeing. "Even when I was the greenest nurse in the ER, people expected me to know what was going on."

"As long as we're analyzing this stereotyping thing," she said, deciding to have a little fun, "we shouldn't leave out that men with eyes the color of freshly brewed coffee are generally perceived to be—"

"Could you believe that woman?" he said, interrupting.

"Of course, you had to be professional here at the office, but if you and Matthew's mom decide to get together—"

"That won't happen," he snapped.

"But it would be nice for young Matthew to have a tall man to look up to."

"Don't you have some place you're supposed to be? Like lunch with your uncle?"

She checked her watch. "Yikes! I'm about to be late."

"Take your time. Your first afternoon appointment cancelled."

"Oh? A new patient or one of Keith's regulars?"

"A regular," he said, concern etching his forehead. "The Logans have four children, and it's not like them to cancel at the last minute."

Beth hurried to her car, wondering why Noah

seemed troubled by the cancellation. It didn't seem odd to her. People had to change their plans all the time.

It was a short drive to Cathedral Hills Country Club, a favorite lunch spot for BMC doctors. The hostess called her by name and said, "Are you dining with a friend today?"

"With my uncle, Dr. Albert Brennan." Beth scanned the dining room, expecting to see her uncle's bald head before the hostess could show her to his table.

The hostess scanned her list of reservations. "Your uncle must not be dining with us today. He has no reservation, and he or his staff always call."

Beth backed away. "I must have misunderstood." While the valet retrieved her car, she called her uncle's receptionist and asked if there had been a change in his luncheon plans.

"Not since I talked to Mona early this morning. I told her that your uncle had decided to take you to The Hilltop. She said she would give you the message."

"No doubt she did. I must have missed it."

"Or she deliberately didn't give it to you," the woman said suspiciously.

Did anyone at BMC have a kind word for Mona? "Would you call my uncle for me and tell him I'm on my way?"

"I sure will. And don't worry. He'll understand."

Would Mona have deliberately withheld a message? Today, the consequence was a mild inconvenience, but another time, it could affect patient care.

Again, Beth left her car with a parking valet and walked inside the plush restaurant. With the best view of the valley and a top chef on staff, The Hilltop was fine dining at its best. If she had known they were eating here, she would have worn something dressier and traded her sneakers for designer pumps. Her mother had taught her what was appropriate even if Beth sometimes chose to ignore it.

Should she touch up her makeup, or did it matter that much when she was already late? She followed the maître d' to a window table where her uncle and another man waited. They stood as they saw her.

"Here's our Bethie," her uncle said, beaming. "I hear you got lost, hon."

"I'm sorry to be late. I don't make it a habit."

"I'm sure you don't. Bethie, I've brought along Zack Hemmingway, the second-best orthopedic surgeon in town."

Zack Hemmingway's eyes shone with intelligence and good humor. She guessed that he was in his midthirties.

"Second-best?" she said, offering her hand. "That's high praise, coming from Uncle Al."

Zack wasn't classically handsome, but in his hand-tailored dark suit, crisp white shirt and expensive silk tie, he had the confident look of a man who could hold his own anywhere.

"You should hear what your uncle says about you." Zack glanced at her footwear and grinned. "He said you'd be wearing yellow sneakers, so everything else must be true."

The maître d' slipped a fine linen napkin out of her goblet and positioned it across her lap with an elegant flourish. The fancier the restaurant, the more likely they were to do that, but it always made her laugh.

Fortunately, it wasn't her piggy laugh.

"When I knew you would be late," her uncle said, "I took the liberty of ordering something for you."

"I'm so glad," she said, as a meal was placed before her. The grilled chicken on a bed of exotic salad greens with edible flowers looked appetizing, but both men had luscious-looking steaks. Hungrily, she eyed Zack's steaming baked potato.

"I think they mixed up our orders," Zack said, picking up his plate and trading it for hers.

She looked at him in surprise.

"Zack, you ordered the steak," her uncle insisted.

"But did you see the way your niece was eyeing it?" he teased. "I used to have a pup who envied every bite. That's too much pressure."

"Now I'm really embarrassed," she said, picking up the plate with the steak and trying to trade back.

Zack waved her off. "Forget it. I'm happy to finally meet a woman in Beverly Hills who eats real food."

"But I can't let you do this."

Smiling, he forked salad greens into his mouth as if they were just what he wanted. "Now, you owe me one, don't you think?"

With her mouth full of buttery baked potato, Beth could only nod. Zack seemed like a highly eligible man, and that's what she was looking for, wasn't it? He'd sacrificed his meal for hers, he didn't seem to mind that he looked a whole lot better than she did and he didn't work in her office. What more could she ask?

Chapter Seven

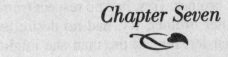

When Noah came back from lunch, Vanessa was on the phone, but she took time out to share big news. Mona had failed to give Beth a message about a location switch for her lunch date, and Beth had shown up very late, which was really bad because her uncle had brought along his protégé, Zack Hemmingway, just to meet Beth.

Noah felt the blood rush to his head. It was only Beth's second day, but Mona was making trouble and Zack Hemmingway was making his move, just as the BMC grapevine had predicted.

If Noah needed orthopedic surgery, he'd want Zack Hemmingway's skill. The man was that good. But Noah didn't want to see Beth used, not by this guy or anyone else.

The grapevine conclusion was that one day Beth's grandfather would turn the reins over to one of his sons. Beth's dad, James T. Brennan, Jr., was the oldest, but he lived for his work. Charles took nothing seriously. Only Al had the ambition to head the clinic, and who would be Al's successor? He had no children.

Charles's son, Collin, had no administrative ambitions. Beth's brother, Trey, had no respect from the staff, and her brother, Ry, had no desire to work here. That left her, or the man she might marry.

If the BMC grapevine had figured that out, it was a sure thing that Zack Hemmingway had.

In theory, Noah didn't care how the Brennan medical dynasty developed, but Beth deserved to be loved for herself, not her name and connections. As intelligent and intuitive as she was, she would figure out what was going on. How would she feel about it? Would she fall for Hemmingway?

"Mona's going to be in so much trouble!" Vanessa was saying to her friend on the phone. "Dr. Beth is just the nicest person, but this is bound to make her mad."

Mona came in and put her purse away. Noah went through the motions of checking the folders of the afternoon patients. Vanessa ended her call, saying, "Thanks for checking in, hon. If there's any change in the…weather, I'll let you know."

She unwrapped a candy from her kangaroo dish and popped it into her mouth with a wink at Noah.

"Really, Vanessa," Mona chided. "It is so unprofessional of you to chitchat with your friends. Keep it up and you could be looking for a new job."

"Mo-na," Vanessa said, drawling the name, "you know, you really do moan a lot."

"You're such a child," Mona said with contempt.

"I'm not the one playing games," Vanessa returned with plenty of sass.

Noah gave Vanessa a silencing look. It would be better to leave Mona's discipline, or better, her dismissal, to their boss. He hoped Beth had the guts to do it.

"Hi, everybody," Beth said, breezing into the office with a smile on her face as she always did, the very picture of a woman content with her life.

Man, what did it take to make Beth upset?

"Did you have a nice lunch?" Mona asked, her voice syrupy sweet.

Beth had to notice that wasn't normal.

"Lunch was the best," Beth enthused. "It was a beautiful day for a drive. I had the top down on my little convertible, and I could have driven around all afternoon. Actually, I almost did."

Hah! Beth wasn't going to let this slide.

"Did you have trouble finding your restaurant?" Mona asked innocently.

"The Hilltop? Oh, not at all. I've been going there since I was a teenager. Did any important messages come in while I was gone, Vanessa?"

"Just these two," Vanessa took pink message forms from the top tray where all messages went. "You were caught up on your messages and callbacks before lunch, Dr. Beth," Vanessa said pointedly.

C'mon, Beth, put it together, he urged silently.

But the look on her face as she glanced over her messages said that she was either incredibly dense or had no spine at all.

She turned and walked toward her office, but said over her shoulder, "Mona, will you join me for a minute?"

Yes! Noah felt a smile coming on. The doc had plenty of spine. There had been no flare of temper that all of them had to endure, no harsh words that might filter out to waiting patients and nothing that would affect office morale. Just quiet words to the target.

Mona strutted down the hall as if she were just spoiling to duke it out with her boss. He whispered to himself, "Let the games begin."

Vanessa muttered, "I think I'll go find a box for Mona to pack her things in."

Beth took her time, trading her blazer for her white lab coat. She'd prayed all the way back to the office and planned to keep Mona's reprimand very low-key.

Slinging her stethoscope around her neck, she sat on the edge of her desk and said pleasantly, "Mona, we all make mistakes. You've been a valued part of Brennan Medical Clinic for many years, so, please, don't worry about the mistake you made today."

"I was here long before you were, *Bethie,*" Mona said, looking down her nose, "and I'll be here after you're gone! I don't make mistakes!"

The menacing power coming out of the woman hit Beth like a physical blow. The Bible said a gentle word was supposed to turn away wrath, but just how much more gentle could she have been? Could she get through to someone with so much hate?

"Mona, it wasn't a huge mistake, but failing to give me the message from my uncle about the change of restaurants *was* a mistake. You and I are in the trust-building stage, and I must know that you don't take this lightly. It was only lunch today, but another time, it might have consequences that neither of us want."

"Don't blame *me* because *you* failed to read *your* messages!" the woman said with a smirk.

The smirk was a dead giveaway. In some obscure

location, Beth *would* find the message, and Mona would claim it was just where it belonged.

"Do you remember where you put the message, Mona?" Beth asked with the patience she would use on a child who'd lost a toy. Granted, it was demeaning, but she'd taken about all of Mona's insolence she could stand.

"Of course, I remember!"

"Why don't you show me?"

"Show you?" Mona practically laughed in her face. "Let me just do that." Pivoting, she marched to the front office and pulled a letter-size sheet of paper from Beth's in-tray, the one reserved for letters and lab reports. "There! There's your message!"

"But Mona," Vanessa said, "we always put the phone messages on the pink forms in the top tray."

"Nothing of the sort. Messages go in both trays."

"Is that a new rule?" Noah asked, making it clear that it wasn't.

Beth never ran from a fight, but she did sidestep a lot. "I'll tell you what," she said. "Let's call this incident a learning experience. To avoid mix-ups, in the future, it's officially a rule. My phone-in messages go on the pink forms and in my top tray."

"Just like we've always done," Vanessa said, taking one last snipe at Mona.

Beth couldn't begrudge her that.

The rest of the afternoon sped by, partly because Beth kept getting phone calls from her family about Mona's message misdirection. Beth took them between patients at the front desk.

Grandpa asked if she needed him to get to the bottom of the message mix-up. Uncle Al said she was putting BMC at risk for a malpractice suit if she didn't get rid of Mona. Uncle Charlie offered to try charming Mona to resign. Collin reported that the grapevine consensus was that Mona should get the ax.

Mona might have felt the heat, because she'd left early for a "dental appointment." Beth pretended not to see Vanessa give Noah a low-five.

When the phone rang again, Beth thought it might be her dad. He was the only Brennan doctor who hadn't checked in. But it was Zack Hemmingway. Beth took the call at the desk, sure that it wouldn't be a long call. They both had patients to see.

Zack said the usual things—he was happy to meet her, he hoped they would see each other again. Because she had an audience, she kept her responses brief, but positive. She could see Zack becoming a good friend.

"Your uncle filled me in on the situation with your nurse," Zack said, sympathetically. "I expect you're getting plenty of advice. Not that anyone has asked for my opinion, but I think you should handle things your way, Beth. You didn't get this far by misdiagnosing problems."

She hadn't expected that. "Thank you, Zack. I really needed to hear that."

The conversation ended, and Vanessa asked, "Is Dr. Hemmingway as nice as I've heard?"

"I don't know what you've heard, but he seems nice."

Noah's quick frown said he was listening and it bothered him. What was that about?

"But then," she added, "I would think any man was nice who gave me his steak and ate my salad instead."

A quick smile crossed Noah's face. He'd liked that.

"You don't mind that Dr. Hemmingway is the bossy type?" Vanessa asked. "Everybody says he's really bossy."

"'Bossy' is part of an orthopod's DNA, Vanessa," Beth said. "They're very particular about their patients' care. That doesn't mean they're bossy with friends."

"People talk about how good-looking he is, but I don't think he's nearly as good-looking as Noah."

"Vanessa!" Noah protested.

"Well, he's not!" Vanessa said, overriding his protest. "Noah, if the two of you were standing side by side, nobody would even look at Dr. Hemmingway."

Noah felt hot color creep up his neck and cover his face. He knew she meant well, but it was embarrassing, having her talk about him that way.

"Vanessa," Beth said quietly. "We're not going to talk about how Noah looks."

"But, Dr. Beth, have you *ever* seen a better-looking man in scrubs than Noah?"

"That's it," he said, heading toward the door.

"Noah, wait." Beth stopped him. "I'm sorry. That won't happen again."

Vanessa looked genuinely perplexed.

"Vanessa, do guys ever talk about your looks?" Beth asked, knowing the answer. Vanessa's Latin beauty would turn heads.

"Does the sun shine in L.A.?" The young woman batted her dramatic dark eyes and struck a fashion pose, one hand on a slender hip. "Of course they do."

"Did you ever mind?"

There was a slight pause before Vanessa's eyes widened. "Oh! I was doing that harassment thing. I'm sorry, Noah. Please, don't sue me."

"Not this time." Noah smiled and mentally chalked up another point for Beth. She'd handled that well.

Vanessa went down the hall to turn off the lights.

"Just for the record," Beth teased softly, so Vanessa wouldn't hear, "she was right. You would win Best Guy in Scrubs, but that's the last time you'll hear it here."

That was nice to know, but still plenty embarrassing. He smiled to be a good sport and turned toward the door as he should have done ten minutes ago.

The phone rang and Beth said, "Office hours are over. The answering service will pick that up."

Even though he'd often walked away from a ringing phone at closing time, this time Noah reached for the phone.

"Daddy!" Kendi practically screamed into the phone.

His heart seemed to stop. "What's the matter, baby?"

"Harlene won't wake up! She can't drink her orange juice or eat her special candy. I don't know what to do."

Noah's heart pounded so hard, he could hardly breathe. "It's my daughter," he told Beth. "Her babysitter is diabetic and unresponsive."

"Have your daughter call 911 and stay on the line with them," Beth said, her words clipped and sure.

"Kendra, listen to me, baby. You're in charge now."

"Harlene's my patient!" his baby said, her voice trembling.

Vaguely, he realized that Beth had disappeared. "Here's what I want you to do. As soon as we hang up, call 911, just like we practiced. Tell the helper who answers about Harlene. Do you remember her address?"

"Yep, two numbers different from ours."

"The 911 helpers will make sure the paramedics find you if you don't hang up. Keep talking and when you hear the siren and know the paramedics are there, unlock the front door. Okay?"

"I can do it."

"I'll be right there, Kendi." He disconnected and ran toward the stairs.

Beth was there at the end of the hall, holding the door of the elevator. "This way, Noah," she said.

She was right. The elevator would be faster.

"Where's your car parked?" she asked crisply.

"I'm in the back lot."

"I'm closer. I'll be at the clinic entrance drive, ready to follow you."

He could hardly believe she would do this, but on the ground floor, she was out of the elevator, running as fast toward her car as he ran toward his.

He flashed his lights when he saw her in a yellow VW convertible at the clinic entrance. He pulled out, keeping her car in his rearview mirror all the way.

As long as he could remember, he'd been a loner who didn't let people into his life. Why then, did he feel such comfort, knowing Beth was behind him?

Beth prayed constantly as she zigzagged in and out of freeway traffic, never losing sight of Noah's car while she thought about what might lie ahead. If Kendra couldn't rouse her babysitter, the woman could be in insulin shock or diabetic coma. That wasn't good, but with prompt treatment she could recover from either.

As a doctor, Beth knew the paramedics were better equipped to handle Harlene's care than she was, but tagging along felt like the right thing to do. Every single parent needed help sometimes.

They entered an older neighborhood of modest homes. Harlene's must be the one with the ambulance parked at curbside. Noah wheeled into an adjacent driveway, and Beth parked in front of a house with pink shutters.

"Dad-dee!" a beautiful little girl screamed as she flew toward Noah.

He scooped her up in his arms.

"Harlene is going to be all better. The par'medics stuck a needle in her arm so they could give her med'cine, and they said I was a good nurse."

Watching the way Noah held his child, his strong arms about her, her head cupped lovingly to his shoulder, Beth felt tears sting her eyes. Had her father ever held her that way?

"I'm proud of you, Kendi," Noah said, giving his little girl a kiss on her forehead. "Good job."

She kissed him back on the forehead as if it were a comforting ritual, shared many times. Noticing Beth, Kendi smiled with the happy confidence of a well-loved child. "Hi. Are you a nurse, like Daddy and me?"

Before Beth could answer, Noah said, "Kendi, this is Dr. Beth. She's the one you've been drawing pictures for."

"I love your pictures!" Beth said, smiling at the adorable little girl even as she stored the image of the two of them in her heart. Every child should have the security of this kind of love.

Noah lowered his daughter to the ground. "Kendi, why don't you stay here and talk to Dr. Beth while I see what I can do to help Harlene."

"Okay," she said, not at all afraid of making a new friend.

Beth knelt so they would be on the same level. "Your daddy calls you Kendi. Do you like that better than Kendra?"

"I like Kendra. Kendi is just Daddy's name for me."

"You are a very smart girl, the way you called 911 and got help for Harlene."

"Yep. Everybody came fast."

"Were you scared when Harlene wouldn't wake up?"

The child nodded, her eyes big. "But I prayed for her. Me and Harlene go to church together and know how to pray."

"That's great." How different her life would have been if someone in her family had known the power of prayer. "You prayed and look what happened! The paramedics came fast, and your dad did, too."

"And you!" Kendra slipped her hand into Beth's, as trusting as if they'd known each other forever.

Noah joined them. "They have Harlene ready for transport. They'll be taking her to Cedar Hills," he said, sounding calm, probably for Kendra's sake, but his eyes flicked anxiously at the medics loading their patient in the ambulance.

"Noah, would you like to follow them and stay with Harlene?" Beth asked, knowing that was what she would want to do if the patient were dear to her.

"Yes, but Kendi—"

"Kendra can hang out with me. Would that be okay?"

"Please! Say yes, Daddy!" Kendra begged.

He hesitated as if he hated to accept such a favor.

"Please!" Beth begged, imitating his daughter so well that he smiled.

"I won't stay long."

"Stay as long as you like. I'll take Kendra to dinner."

"Daddy!" Kendra exclaimed with awed delight, catching sight of Beth's car. "Dr. Beth has a yellow car!"

"She sure does, and look at her shoes."

"Yellow sneakers! Dr. Beth, you're duh bomb!" the child said, jumping up and down.

"Kendra, you have a yellow dress. *You're* duh bomb!" The jumping thing Beth could have managed, but not in front of Noah and the emergency medics.

"I guess I don't have to worry about the two of you bonding," Noah said dryly as he slid into his car. "Kendi, be a good girl for Dr. Beth. Show her where we have the house key and wash up before you go to dinner. I really appreciate this, Beth."

Their eyes met, and she said, "I'll be praying, Noah."

A muscle twitched in his jaw, and he looked away. "Harlene would like that." And then he was gone.

Chapter Eight

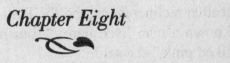

Kendra gave Beth the tour of her modest home like a gracious little hostess. Noah was a very tidy guy. Nothing was out of place, no laundry waited to be done, no dishes sat in the sink. The floors and surfaces seemed spotless, and all of Kendra's clothes were neatly folded and stored.

Beth knew what it took to keep things looking this way, and she had to wonder how a single parent did it all. "Your house is very nice, Kendra," she said, curiosity pushing her to nose into their personal life just a bit. "It's so clean! Who does all this work?"

"Me and Daddy play a game called Cleaning House. We play lots of games, but that's my fav'rite. I *love* to clean. Sometimes I beat him and win."

A man who made life fun for his child and

taught her a great work ethic—that was every woman's dream.

"Mommy's fav'rite color was pink," Kendi reported needlessly.

It looked as if little had changed from the way Kendra's mother left it. Except for the black leather recliner facing the TV, Beth wouldn't have known a man lived here. "Your mommy *really* liked pink," she said.

"Yep. This was her pink Bible." From a table by the sofa, Kendra handed it to Beth. "My Bible's at Harlene's. We read it together. It's the kind for children, but someday I'm going to have a yellow one."

"What color is Daddy's Bible?" Beth asked, admittedly a little nosy.

"He doesn't have one. Daddy says he hears all the stories from me, so he doesn't have to read them himself."

As a person who'd only read the Bible the last two years herself, Beth could hardly think badly of Noah for that, but he was missing one of the great blessings in life.

Kendra took her mother's Bible and put it back exactly where it had been. "Me and Daddy keep everything like it was when Mommy lived here."

That sounded so sad. Did Noah keep it this

way for Kendra's sake? Or was their home a shrine because he wasn't ready to move on?

Beth followed Kendra to her bedroom and noticed the very feminine way Noah's wife had decorated. None of it would have been Beth's choice, but she'd never been a woman who loved shopping for makeup, jewelry, purses and shoes— not that she sometimes didn't wish she were more like that.

"This is my bed," Kendra said proudly, sitting on the edge of the small white bed, carefully made up, complete with fluffy pillows and little stuffed animals.

"It's beautiful, Kendra. You must like flowers." They were everywhere—on her bedding, the walls, even the ceiling.

"I love flowers! My mommy did, too. This is her." She handed a framed picture to Beth.

"She's beautiful."

"Yep. Like me."

Beth smiled. She'd never been that confident of her looks, but then, at her house, praise came for making straight A's or the tennis team.

"You have your mommy's eyes," she said softly, noticing the unusual lavender-blue.

Kendra nodded. "But I got yellow hair."

In the picture, Kendra's mother's long dark hair curled around a heart-shaped face. Lush, dark eyelashes accented gorgeous eyes. Noah had married a very beautiful woman.

"I'm going to show you something very special," Kendra said, opening a tiny box. "This is my diamond ring." It was a toy ring with an outrageously big "diamond."

"Wow!" Beth said, reacting with the appreciation such a prize deserved. "Is this a special ring?"

"Yep. Daddy says I can have my mommy's diamond ring when I grow up, but I have this one for now. I keep it in the box 'cause I don't want to lose it."

A lump grew in Beth's throat as the reality of this little family's loss sunk in. She'd often seen bad things happen to good people, and she knew the scripture, "all things work together for good to those who love the Lord," but it took faith to believe the loss of a loved one could be part of God's plan for this precious child and her dad.

The drive-in diner had a fifties theme with roller-skating food servers and Elvis tunes playing through the speakers. With the top down on the VW, Beth and Kendra moved to the music and munched their way through dinner.

"This is my fav'rite place," Kendra said, happy as a child can be. "I'm gonna work here when I get big."

"You'll be good at it. I expect you'll be good at a lot of things."

Kendra nodded. "Yep."

For such a little girl, she had held up her end of the conversation better than many adults. The way she talked about her parents, though, almost broke Beth's heart. Noah must have reminded Kendra of the good times repeatedly, or she wouldn't have these stories to tell. For sure, she wouldn't have remembered her baby years, and she wouldn't have such absolute assurance of her mother's love.

Stowing their used napkins and paper containers into a sack, Beth watched Kendra dip her last French fry into ketchup and pop it in her mouth. She hadn't eaten all of her hot dog, but the chocolate shake was history.

Beth's cell phone rang, and she answered it.

"Beth, this is Noah."

Her heart rate picked up just the way it used to when she'd get a call from the cute boy in class. "How are things going for Harlene?" she asked, grateful that her mind remembered what was important even if her body didn't.

"Good, but they're admitting her."

"That's best. Are you planning to stay with her?"

He hesitated before saying, "I don't like the

idea of leaving Harlene when she has no one else, but…" His voice trailed off as if he hated asking for a bigger favor.

That wasn't the way she thought of it. "I would love to have Kendra sleep over at my place."

"Sleep over?" the child said, picking up on Beth's half of the conversation. Her face radiated joy.

"Only if your daddy says you can."

"Please, Daddy," Kendra pleaded loudly enough for him to hear as well as the diners beside them.

"But you have rounds," he said.

She'd thought of that. "You could watch Kendra while I do rounds, then I'll take her for the night?"

"I can't believe you're doing this. I mean, I've only worked with you for two days, and you're helping me out."

"I'm helping you out? Well, it's nice that you think that, but I'm having a wonderful time with my new friend! Besides—" She turned her head away from Kendra and lowered her voice. "Noah, you helped me out on the worst day of my life, and you didn't know me at all."

It was just like old times for Noah, eating an unappetizing dinner in the hospital cafeteria with one eye on the clock, ever mindful that he needed to get back to the floor. Staying with Harlene in the ER, being part of the frenetic pace, getting her settled into her room—all of it came as naturally as breathing. He'd missed the hospital environment more than he'd realized.

Kendra sat across from him, playing with her straw more than drinking her juice, but, as Beth had warned him, Kendi couldn't possibly be hungry. In the last minute or so, his talkative daughter had gone strangely silent. There was a wistful look on her little face that made him wonder what was going on. "Whatcha thinkin' about, puddin'?"

She looked away and said softly, "I like Dr. Beth."

"I'm sure she likes you, too." He'd seen the loving way Beth looked at his daughter when she'd left to do rounds.

"I liked riding in her car."

"It's a very cool car."

"I liked talking to her."

"She's fun to talk to."

"It was like being with Mommy."

The air rushed out of Noah's lungs, and he bent his head so Kendi wouldn't see how her sweet words pained him.

It wasn't the first time his daughter's sadness triggered a surge of grief, and he was terribly afraid it wouldn't be the last. It was a helpless feeling, not being able to make it better for Kendi, but what could he do?

He'd already changed jobs. He'd kept their routine as nearly the same as possible. He'd made Kendi the center of his life. Short of bringing Merrilee back, what was left? If he knew, he'd do anything, make any sacrifice. That's what a good dad did.

"Do you think Dr. Beth would play with me sometime when Harlene's not in the hospital?" Kendi asked wistfully.

"I'm sure she would." The instinct to lighten his baby's heart was stronger than common sense. Beth was a generous person who reached out and loved everyone in her path, but he'd grown up knowing about boundaries and when they couldn't be crossed. Logic said his daughter wouldn't have the opportunity to build a relationship with his boss.

In fact, if it weren't for his promise to the senior Dr. Brennan, he'd be looking for another job. Beth only had to glance at him for his heart rate to pick up, his mouth to go dry and his concentration to falter. He'd even dreamed about her last night.

Ironically, he couldn't think how Beth made any of that happen. It wasn't that she flirted or played the age-old games women played. She never let on that she saw him as anything more than her office nurse and new friend.

That was all he was, and all he wanted to be. There was no reason he should mind that she hadn't noticed him as a man, but he did…just a bit…

Okay, it bothered him a lot. But it shouldn't. A sensible guy removed himself from a no-win situation. A new job—that's what he needed.

A yellow-sneaker-wearing woman bounced into the cafeteria, like a burst of sunshine on a cold, rainy day.

"Beth!" his child cried, waving both arms wildly. "Over here!"

The sight of Beth was all it took to put the joy back in his little girl's face. He knew the feeling. It was incredible how the sight of one pretty blonde could make such a difference.

Beth waved back and the corners of her mouth lifted in his favorite smile. "Is there anyone here who wants to see my condo?" she asked as if she didn't know the answer.

"Me!" Kendi wiggled out of her chair, grabbed Beth's hand and pulled her toward the door.

"Hold up a minute," Beth said, laughing as she reined Kendi in and wrapped her in a hug, facing Noah. "We need to talk to your dad before we go."

"Why?" his child said impatiently, ready to leave.

Noah couldn't believe it. Kendra hadn't spent a night away from him since he'd started working days. They never parted company without a hug and a kiss, yet she could leave without a backward glance?

"We're going to ask your dad for last-minute instructions. He's the boss, you know."

A look of mutiny crossed his child's face, not an attractive sight. Maybe he'd let her become too strong-willed, but he wanted her to grow up to be a strong woman capable of making good decisions. As wonderful as Merrilee had been, she couldn't say no when she'd needed to, and she'd paid for that mistake with her life.

"Kendi has a suitcase," he said, "and she'll need—"

"I know what I need," his self-assured child said.

They really were going to have to work on this.

"But my backpack is at Harlene's, Daddy. I'll need it for school."

"We'll take care of that in the morning when I take you to school," he said, concerned at how grown-up his baby was acting. It had better be acting.

"I can take Kendra to school if it turns out you need to stay," Beth offered.

"Yay!" Kendi jumped up and down with the

bubbly enthusiasm he knew so well. Usually, he was the one to make her happy like that.

"Kendi, if I have to stay that means Harlene isn't getting well," he admonished.

"Oh," she said, much more subdued.

Beth jotted her home address on a prescription pad, ripped it off and handed it to him. "This is where we'll be." She bent over and whispered something in Kendi's ear.

Kendi looked into Beth's eyes and nodded. Leaving Beth's arms, she came over, climbed into his lap and threw her arms around him in a big hug.

That was more like it. He loved holding his baby.

She swished her long hair aside, put her hands on either side of his face and planted a kiss on his forehead, just like always. "You be a good boy, Dad. If you need me, I'll be at Dr. Beth's."

It felt as if they'd just turned a corner, and there was no going back. He watched them leave, hand in hand, already having a good time…without him.

"You look like you just lost your best friend," Glenda Shepherd said, setting her dinner tray on his table. She'd worked with him as an ER nurse, and she'd known Merrilee, too.

"I'm in shock," he admitted. "My daughter just left to spend her first night away from me, and she was…happy about it."

"C'mon, Noah! Don't tell me you're one of those parents who thinks your child's life revolves around you."

What was wrong with that?

"I noticed that your friend, Harlene, was admitted," Glenda said, twirling spaghetti onto her fork.

He nodded and glanced at his watch. "I ought to get back."

"Stay a couple of minutes. I haven't seen you since Collin and I were engaged." She held out her left hand, flashing a very big diamond. "What do you think of the rock?"

"Cool ring! Kendi has a diamond that big, but hers came with a necklace and stick-on earrings."

"Maybe Collin will give me those for our anniversary."

She could always make him smile. "Seriously, it's a beautiful ring and very impressive, especially from a doc who's not that long out of med school."

"Yeah, but the Brennan kids don't have medical school debt. They wouldn't have to work a day in their lives to hang out with the rich and famous."

"And you're cool with that?"

She smiled ruefully. "Not all the time, but I love Collin. It's not his fault he's a Brennan. How are you getting along with the Brennan princess?"

"Don't call her that," he said, instantly annoyed.

"Then she's not spoiled rotten, like people say?"

"No! She's terrific!"

"That's what Collin said, but I figured he was prejudiced. So, who was the cute blonde walking out with your daughter? I hope that means you're seeing someone."

"That was Beth Brennan."

"You're kidding! Can you believe she's one of my bridesmaids, and I haven't even met her?"

"You'll like her a lot. She's really sweet."

"Are you going to use her as Kendra's pediatrician?"

"Absolutely. Beth's as good as any peds doc I've worked with—maybe better than Jordahl. She makes an office visit fun for a kid."

"Is she going to make *your* life fun, Noah?"

"I think so! She lets us give the kids lollipops *and* stickers."

"Then you ought to do something nice for her. Be her escort at our wedding? I know she's not paired with anyone yet, and all of Collin's groomsmen are married."

"Believe me, Glenda. You don't have to set Beth up."

"But you two would be perfect together. You're

tall, dark and not too bad-looking; she's blond and really cute."

"I already have a date for your wedding. She's blond and really cute, too."

"But your cute blonde shares your DNA. Bring 'em both. From the way Kendra skipped out of here with her new friend, I'd say she would love to have Beth along."

He hadn't dated in years, but what woman wanted a guy to bring his daughter along?

"Collin says Zack Hemmingway's already made his move, and I saw her talking to Luke Jordahl yesterday. I wouldn't be surprised if they didn't both ask her. Beat 'em to it, Noah. You'll be doing her a favor."

That much was true. He didn't want to see her with either one of those doctors.

"You're hedging? Okay, what's wrong, Noah? What are you hiding?"

"I'm not hiding anything. It's just…Beth is my boss. Even if she weren't, she'd still be a doctor."

"And what's wrong with that?" Glenda bristled. "You're not saying that doctors and nurses shouldn't get together, I hope."

"No, of course not."

She blew on her diamond and buffed it against her shirt. "That's reassuring. I'd hate to give this gorgeous thing back. So, it's all right for a female nurse to fall for a male doctor, but a male nurse can't fall for a female doc? Noah! That's so old school!"

"I know." He wouldn't argue the point, nor would he admit he liked everything about Beth, from her caramel-colored eyes to her sassy yellow sneakers. He loved the way her mind worked and the way she handled people.

But he came from nothing and struggled to pay his bills. She had everything and worked because she wanted to. His address might be only miles away from hers, but they were worlds apart.

Beth watched Kendra pack her little suitcase, thinking that this was the second time she'd been in Noah's house without him being there. It was a strange feeling, trespassing on his privacy, even if it was for a good cause.

"All done!" Kendra said, zipping the case. "I have my princess nightie, clothes for school, one toy animal, my hairbrush, my toothbrush. Oh, I forgot. My toothpaste!"

"I have toothpaste you can use, Kendra."

"That's okay, mine is for children. It tastes like watermelon!"

In her work Beth had seen children with many personalities and many behaviors, but she'd never seen one more self-sufficient than this little girl.

That spoke well of her parents. Confidence like Kendra's didn't develop overnight.

"Here it is," Kendra sang as she skipped back into the room. "Oh, I should take my paper and markers. I'll make another picture for you."

"That would be great."

Kendra pulled out a box from the bottom of her closet and knelt on the floor. "These are some of my pictures."

Beth knelt beside her and admired her drawings. Kendra had repeatedly drawn one subject, then moved on to repeatedly draw another, creating a journal of her development.

There were many versions of a single flower with differently colored petals. There was a whole series of tulips, and another series of rainbows, all with the yellow stripe a bit wider than the other colors.

But one series brought tears to Beth's eyes. In each picture, a woman wore a pink dress. She had long dark hair, blue eyes and eyelashes drawn like the legs of a spider. Her mouth was red in some pictures, pink or orange in others.

These would have been drawn soon after her mother died.

"Those are pictures of my mommy," the child said unnecessarily.

"She is so pretty, Kendra."

Kendra nodded. "Like me. And you!"

"Sweetie, I'm not pretty like your mommy."

"Yes, you are! You have yellow hair like me."

"But yours is long and beautiful."

"You can let your hair grow, and we can be the same. Daddy likes long hair…and dresses. He really likes dresses."

This little girl was mommy-shopping! Beth gathered the artwork and put it back in the box. There was a lump in her throat put there by tears held checked. She wished she could be what Kendra wanted. Every child needed a mom.

Could she fall for Noah? Those broad shoulders and intense brown eyes got her attention, but it was his kindness and the selfless way he took care of Kendra and Harlene that touched her heart.

But, bottom line, she wasn't growing her hair long, she wasn't switching to dresses and she would never be as tidy as he was. Since they worked together, it was just as well that she wasn't his kind of woman because he was definitely her kind of man.

Chapter Nine

Beth sipped coffee in the kitchen and watched Kendra on the balcony. The little girl pretended to be the queen while giving her toy animal a lesson in manners. It was a two-in-one game that kept Kendra busy while Beth cleaned up their breakfast dishes without the child's help.

If Kendra realized Beth was doing something she could participate in, the little girl would be right there to assist. She was not a child to watch from the sidelines, and she had the confidence to try anything.

Beth could easily imagine her tagging along with Noah as he kept their home tidy and clean. It was a lot of responsibility for one parent.

Queen Kendra wore a necklace of big, bright-colored beads—the only item deemed worthy from Beth's meager collection of jewelry—and a crown Beth had made of aluminum foil. Her pink dress, scattered with flowers, had been a present from Daddy.

Beth smiled, imagining that tall, broad-shouldered shopper in the little girl's department, pushing dress hangers on the clothes rack, looking for a dress in his daughter's favorite colors—yellow, pink, purple and blue, in that exact order of preference.

The doorbell rang, and Kendra called, "Is that Daddy?"

"Probably." Beth carried her coffee to the door and peered through the security peephole. A blast of attraction hit her powerfully. How could a sleepy-eyed man with an overnight growth of beard look so good?

She opened the door and said, "How's Harlene?"

"Better. Well enough to kick me out," he said with a sheepish grin.

Running from the balcony, Kendra sang out in a sweet little voice, "Good morn-ing to my dad-dee."

Noah gave Beth an apprehensive glance, but sang back, "Good morn-ing to my pud-din.'"

His raspy baritone put goose bumps on Beth's arms—the kind she usually got when a tenor hit a high note. "Wow!" She didn't mean to say that. It slipped out.

"Kind of silly, huh?" he said softly.

"Kind of wonderful!" She would have loved it if her dad had been that "silly."

"It's the way we begin every day," he said, almost apologetically, picking up Kendra and planting a kiss on her forehead. She held his cheeks and returned that kiss.

Beth just melted. She loved their little ritual, and it impressed her a lot that he'd sung his morning greeting as usual, risking embarrassment rather than his daughter's disappointment. How great was that? "Coffee?" she asked, holding up her mug.

He waved away the offer. "I've had plenty."

"How about breakfast?"

"I'll grab something at home."

Kendra took Beth's hand and said, "We need another bowl. Daddy likes this kind of cereal."

"That's okay, Kendi," Noah said, remaining near the door. "We need to go. I've got to get ready for work."

"I don't think you'll be in trouble if you're late today," Beth said, trying to put him at his ease. She got out a bowl and spoon.

"Out here, Daddy." Kendi beckoned him to the balcony.

"Go on. Join her," Beth said. "Make yourself at home. I've already done that at your house. Twice!"

"And I appreciate that." He looked around as he headed toward the balcony. "Nice place!"

"But not as tidy as yours," she teased, bringing milk and fruit to the table.

Kendra filled Noah's bowl with cereal, put it in front of him and scrambled onto her own chair.

"You can go ahead and eat, Daddy. Beth and I already prayed—" She stopped, looked at Noah with serious eyes and explained, "Dr. Beth *told* me to call her just Beth."

He nodded parentally. "That's fine, then."

"She's *Beth* 'cause we're good friends."

He glanced at Beth. "First names are more friendly."

She shrugged happily, acknowledging her own words.

"Beth is my bestest friend, Daddy."

"That's good, sweetheart. Beth has been really nice to you and me."

"I'm Daddy's bestest friend, Beth."

Noah closed his eyes for half a second. Beth knew that look from years of working with families. Parents needed a deep well of patience.

"You're my best *daughter,* sweetheart," he said.

Beth gave him a mental thumbs-up for the perfect response. He'd corrected Kendra's concept of relationships and her grammar.

"Kendra fixed breakfast for me, too," Beth said, jumping in to keep the conversation going.

"I fixed breakfast," Kendra said proudly, "and

you did the praying! Daddy, Beth and me take turns. I prayed for our hot dogs last night, and she prayed for breakfast!"

He looked at Beth "As you've probably figured out, Kendra's the official pray-er at our house."

He seemed uncomfortable about that. She thought it was great that he would give his child such a good upbringing. "When I was growing up, we didn't have an official pray-er at our house. Nobody prayed...ever."

"Didn't you go to church?" Kendra asked Beth incredulously.

"Sometimes I went to church with my friend Meg and her family, but they didn't go all the time."

"I go *all* the time," Kendra said proudly. "Me and Harlene. And Daddy is a good boy and takes us and picks us up when church is over."

"Daddy *is* a good boy," Beth agreed.

The good boy studied the bottom of his cereal bowl, but then, his child had just ratted him out.

"Do you go to church, Beth?" Kendra asked.

"Every Sunday. Wouldn't miss it!"

"Me neither!"

"And what does Daddy do between his chauffeuring duties?" she teased, leaning toward Noah.

He turned his head slowly and looked her straight in the eye. "Daddy has time all by himself.

He runs along a path where Kendi's bike can't go. He does whatever he wants for a full hour and a half."

"It sounds as if Daddy really needs that hour and a half," she said sympathetically.

"Daddy…"

They'd left Kendra out of the conversation for fifteen seconds. That was too long. No matter how much Noah adored her—and, clearly, he did—that would be wearing.

"What, pud-din'?"

"Do you like your cereal?"

He'd barely tasted it. Beth noticed.

"It's good, huh?" he said, giving his daughter a smile.

Another great response. If she'd had affirmations like that as a child, would it have taken her thirty years to know what she wanted in life?

Kendra smiled and sighed contentedly. "I like this. It's like we're a family."

Beth glanced at Noah. His eyes were on his cereal bowl, but he was blushing from the neck up. If she were prone to blushing, she would be doing the same thing.

"Hey! I got a good idea!" Kendra was so happy, she bounced in her chair. "Beth, you can have pizza with us Friday night!"

Noah looked too startled to speak.

"We have pizza every Friday night." Kendra's eyes sparkled with anticipation. "You can come with us, Beth."

She would love that. An evening with them would be something to look forward to. Beth waited for Noah to second the invitation.

He shifted uncomfortably in his chair. "Kendi, Friday is only a couple of days away. Beth may have other plans."

Was that classic male evasion or had he given her an escape route to save Kendra's feelings?

"Can you have pizza with us, Beth?" Kendra said hopefully.

It wasn't in Beth to disappoint a child, but it also wasn't in her to go where she wasn't wanted. If Noah wanted her along, he had to say so in a straightforward way.

When he remained silent, she said, "I think I'm supposed to be with other friends that night." Meg and she had planned to get together sometime during the weekend, but they hadn't set a time. Her answer left a loophole if Noah spoke up with a real invitation.

"Kendi, we really need to leave," he said, standing, "or we'll both be late this morning."

He carried his dishes to the kitchen, rinsed them and started to stack them in the dishwasher, but she stopped him. "You don't have to do the dishes."

"Sorry. I must have been on autopilot."

"Don't apologize for a good habit!"

"Beth, about having pizza," he spoke too softly for Kendra to hear, "I've tried to teach Kendi to check with me before she does things, even issuing a pizza invitation to a friend. She's so much like her mother—generous, kind, ready to help—but I want Kendi to learn caution…and to think before she acts."

"I understand," she said, "and I'm glad you told me. You did the right thing."

You did the right thing. The phrase looped in Noah's mind, and he nicked himself shaving. Had it been the right thing to deny Kendi the pleasure of Beth's company this Friday night? Was he wrong to put a halt on a relationship that had no future?

"Daddy, we're going to be late," Kendi said, coming to the bathroom door as she had every two minutes.

Since the school bus had come and gone, he was her transportation to school this morning.

It would make him even more late to work. Beth wouldn't mind, but he couldn't afford to lose time, and he needed to be there to keep an eye on Mona.

"Daddy, I've been thinking."

He wiped his face clean and slapped on the aftershave Harlene had given him for his birthday.

"Why can't Beth have pizza with us Friday night?"

"For one reason, you invited her without checking with me first. We've talked about that."

"If I say I'm sorry and won't do it again, can Beth have pizza with us Friday night?"

He dried the sink area, hung his towel on the rack, snagged the top of his fresh scrubs from the door hook and slipped it over his head. He hated to disappoint her, but it had to be done. "I don't think so, sweetheart."

"Dr. Beth would love Sluggers pizza."

"Maybe you can take her there sometime. She's your friend. Friday is our time. Just you and me."

He headed for the back door, knowing she would follow.

She grabbed up her backpack and trailed him to the car. "Daddy, Beth is our friend."

"But she's also my boss, Kendra. I don't think we should hang out with my boss."

"She's not *my* boss."

Nobody was his daughter's boss, but they were working on that.

"Daddy, Jesus wants us to have friends."

Who needed church when he had his daughter

to preach? He opened the car door for her and waited for her to clamber in and lock her seat belt.

"I have lots of friends, Daddy, but you only have Harlene and me."

That's all he had time for, but he wouldn't lay that guilt trip on Kendi.

"Pleeease, can Beth have pizza with us?"

"Kendra, it will be you and I having pizza at Sluggers, or it will be you and I having red beans and rice at home."

She shuddered in disgust, showing what she thought of his alternative menu. The one time he'd tried cooking Merrilee's Cajun specialty, Kendi had disliked it so much it had been an effective threat ever since.

It worked this time, too. On the drive to school, she didn't mention pizza with Beth again. Or talk to him, not even when she got out of the car.

That sure didn't feel like the right thing.

At the clinic, he arrived just in time to hear Mona chastise Beth in the hall outside Exam Three.

"You cannot wear these silly hats and expect anyone to take you seriously," Mona said, gesturing to the grinning green frog on Beth's head.

Its plastic feet clung to the sides of her head, acting as stabilizers. How could Mona complain when their boss looked so cute?

"The amount of patients you've inherited from Dr. Crabtree is a tribute to his excellence, but, you, Beth Brennan, are ruining his practice!"

"It's my practice to ruin," Beth said reasonably. "Mona, you obviously disapprove of my style of practicing medicine. Life's too short to be upset all the time. I appreciate how loyal you've been to the clinic, but you don't have to stay."

"I most certainly do! Somebody has to make sure you don't run this practice into the ground!"

Whoa! That was uncalled for. "Hey," he called so Beth would know he was standing by.

"It's about time you got here," Mona said, brushing past him. "Vanessa's late, too. You'll have to handle the office alone. I'm going for coffee."

"Have a donut, Mona," he said, just for her ears. "Sweeten up, or people will think you're a grouch."

"Oh, that's lovely," she said sarcastically. "I want things done in a professional manner, and *I'm* to blame? This disrespect never happened when Dr. Crabtree was here."

Mona slammed the door on her way out.

"It's only the third day," Beth said wearily. "I tell myself, it's going to get better."

Noah didn't think so, but Beth was calling the shots. If she had the patience to wait for Mona to show her respect, he could hang in there and be supportive. "I like your hat, by the way."

"So did three-year-old Graysen Drezek, and I liked his mom. We're going to have lunch one of these days. Stacee Drezek said Mona hinted that I was just Keith's temporary replacement."

That blew his mind. "His *temporary* replacement?"

"I don't know which is worse—that Mona might believe it or that she voiced that belief."

"What are you going to do?"

"I don't know. To begin with, I'll pray about it."

Prayer. Right. That sounded like something Merrilee would have said. If Beth wasn't going to tell her grandfather about this, he had to. That was his job.

"I probably shouldn't tell you this, but my family has been pushing me to let Mona go."

When he already knew that, it felt odd not saying so, but how would she feel, knowing her grandfather had asked him to keep an eye on Mona? "Maybe you *should* let her go."

Beth shook her head regretfully. "I don't want to begin this job by costing Mona hers. I want to prove to her—and myself—that Jesus' love is big enough to handle any situation."

Noah used to hear that kind of thing when he went to church with Merrilee. It sounded good in theory, but it didn't work in real life.

When Vanessa returned, Noah brought her up to

speed on the situation with Mona. She was just as uneasy with Beth depending on prayer as he was.

"If Mona's going to talk bad about Dr. Beth, I'm going to talk good!" Vanessa said, determination in her dark eyes.

The moment Mona walked back into the office, Vanessa crooned, "Have you ever seen a doctor who loves babies as much as Dr. Beth?"

He could follow her lead. "You should see how she plays with them when she does the exam. She's as thorough as Dr. Crabtree ever was, but Beth enjoys her job."

That earned him a killing glare from Mona. Perfect.

"It's just precious, how sweet Beth is with the little kids, too," Vanessa gushed.

He couldn't gush. "She's cool with the teens, too."

"Have you noticed how well she keeps on schedule?" Vanessa asked, pouring it on.

Good one, Vanessa! The schedule had been a problem for Crabtree, and it had always annoyed Mona. "I have noticed," he agreed, "and it knocks me out how she can do that without seeming rushed."

"I love it how she never talks down to anyone, even when they're stupid." Vanessa turned toward Mona and aimed that one directly.

His turn. "I love it how she puts the parents at ease. In fact, I've never worked with a better doc."

Vanessa slid him a secret low-five.

The sugar-sweet jabs at Mona weren't particularly mature, but they were complete truths, and Noah felt righteous, establishing his allegiance to Beth.

Maybe it did some good. Mona kept her hateful remarks to herself for the rest of the morning and well into the afternoon. It was so unlike her that Noah waited for the other shoe to drop.

One of the last patients of the afternoon was Beth's nephew, Trey's two-year-old son. Noah had done the intake and left Beth with little J.T. and his mother, Isabel, when the lobby door burst open.

"Where's my son?" Trey Brennan demanded, his face flushed with anger.

"In Exam Two," Mona said promptly, as if she'd been expecting Trey.

Trey dashed down the hall as if a Code Blue had been called. Noah sprinted to catch up. If Beth needed an ally, he was the man for the job.

But Trey came barreling out of the exam room, his toddler in his arms, meeting Noah face-to-face. "Get out of my way, Noah!"

Noah didn't budge. "Is there a problem, doctor?"

"Trey!" his wife pleaded, tugging on his arm. "Don't."

"Izzie, I told you not to bring my son here, and I meant it. Move, Noah."

Not in this lifetime. "You're scaring your son, doctor."

"That's not your business." He shoved against Noah.

He'd have to do better than that. Noah stood firm, blocking his exit. "There are people in the waiting room, doctor. Is this what you want them to see?"

Tears ran down J.T.'s face as he screamed and held out his hands to his mother.

Beth's green frog hat tilted when she grabbed her brother's other arm. "Trey, let's talk about this calmly."

Roughly, he pushed her away.

"You don't want to do that again," Noah said, crowding Trey's space. If it weren't for the baby, he would take the guy out, here and now.

"When I want your opinion, I'll ask for it, Nurse Noah," Trey said nastily.

"Trey, at least use the door in my office," Beth's voice shook with emotion. "No one should see you like this. You're acting crazy."

"What's all this noise?" Beth's grandfather limped through the lobby door. "And why is my namesake so upset?"

"J.T. wants his mother," Vanessa said from her

desk. Her satisfied expression said she'd been the one to call for reinforcements. Had Dr. Brennan asked Vanessa to keep an eye on the situation here, too?

The old man leaned on his cane, his eyes narrow with disgust. "Trey, unless you want people to think you're as unbalanced as your mother, I'd say you'd better give that baby back to Isabel."

That was a low blow, but Trey had asked for it. The guy looked so unstable that Noah backed closer to the senior doctor, ready to keep him from harm.

Little J.T.'s sobs were out of control, and his breath came in spasms.

"Trey, this is too much for J.T. Think what's best for him," Beth begged.

"It's not you! That's for sure."

"We don't have to decide that today," she said more calmly than Noah could have managed.

"'We' won't decide it at all." Trey said, his face menacingly close to hers.

"Trey, give that baby back to his mother," the senior Brennan repeated, his voice steely with authority. "Now!"

Noah thought how angry he would be if someone gave him orders about Kendi. Would Trey defy the chief?

"If you want to keep your office here," Dr.

Brennan added, "you'll treat my doctors with respect. All of my doctors…your sister included."

"But look at this office! And look at my sister! She has a frog on her head! She doesn't belong here, and you know it."

Ooh, bad choice of words, but Dr. Brennan could level people bigger than Trey.

"Trey, if you don't want to be hauled out of here in restraints, you'll hand that poor baby over to Isabel. Get yourself some help before you end up like your mother."

Chapter Ten

Beth sat on the sofa in her grandfather's office, just as she had a year and a half ago. She'd left not knowing why she was going or whether she'd come back. Now, it seemed as if the Lord had planned it that way. She didn't know then that God's plan can be impossible to see.

This evening, she was here to evaluate her first week at BMC, and the first thing she wanted to say was how grateful she was that Grandpa had kept his word. He'd backed her up and encouraged her to be as eccentric as she wanted.

Strangely, her individuality didn't appear to be the point of conflict she'd expected. As her sister-in-law, Isabel, said, it took more than funny hats, yellow sneakers and a VW to qualify as eccentric in Beverly Hills.

Except for her problems with Mona and Trey,

she'd gotten along with the family and the BMC staff fine, and she loved private practice. Not only did she have less people to answer to, she had free time. It was as though she'd been given a free pass to life and didn't know what to do first.

"Sorry to keep you waiting," Grandpa said, shuffling into the room, leaning on his cane.

"Sit down, Grandpa. What can I get you?" As many hours as he spent in his office, he'd furnished it with a small refrigerator, and his office assistant kept it stocked with beverages, fruit and sandwich supplies.

"I think I'd rather wait and have an early dinner. I could use some company. Do you have dinner plans, darling?"

"Not unless they're with you."

"You would spend Friday night with your old grandpa?"

"With pleasure! I did get an invitation from someone younger, but it fell through."

"Someone's loss is my gain," he said, sinking down beside her on the sofa.

"Noah's little girl invited me to share their pizza night…but Noah un-invited me." She'd hoped right up until their last patient left that Noah would change his mind and ask her to join them.

Grandpa frowned. "It's not like Noah to be rude."

"He wasn't rude. It was some kind of lesson for his daughter, something about not being impulsive. It might have been related to his wife's death." She hadn't listened well because she'd been thinking he was just too polite to say she wasn't his type.

"You must not know how Noah's wife died."

"Do you?"

"I got a firsthand account from Stan Calloway, my old golfing buddy. He knew Merrilee McKnight from church and was with her the day she died."

"What happened?" Maybe she would understand Noah better if she knew this.

"Stan and Merrilee McKnight were talking as they walked out of a grocery store, and this disheveled young woman approached them, saying her boyfriend was going to kill her. She needed to get away fast."

"That sounds like a setup."

"Stan thought so. He pulled out his phone and said he would call 911 and stay with her until help arrived. But the woman turned to Merrilee, frantic, sobbing, begging for a ride. Stan strongly advised against it, but soft-hearted Merrilee said she thought Jesus would want her to help the woman."

"Stan offered help."

"Exactly. But Merrilee got suckered in and let the woman into her car. An accomplice overpowered Merrilee and administered a fatal blow to her head. Merrilee was dead at twenty-six. Kendra and Noah's lives were changed forever."

"That certainly explains why Noah wants Kendra to learn caution."

"Indeed."

"Grandpa, on the day of my reception a year and a half ago, you sent Noah to bring me to your office. Why him?"

"It was Keith Crabtree's idea."

"But why would Keith do that?"

"You were always special to him, Beth. He saw how your mother treated you children. Trey became a bully, Ry became a rebel, but you were this tough little girl who wouldn't let anything get her down."

"I wasn't tough. I just learned to stay away."

He pulled her over, and she leaned her head on his shoulder as she had many times before.

"While you were at school, Keith kept tabs on you. He knew how great you were with kids and how much you love your work. At the reception, when I announced that you were coming aboard, I didn't say you were his chosen successor or that he was retiring because that's the way he wanted it—but he was proud of you, darling."

That made her feel ten feet tall. She wanted to thank him, but it wouldn't be easy considering he'd retired to a South Sea island far away from everything and everyone.

"When the others were watching your mother act out, Keith was watching you. He saw you were in trouble, and he sent a man whose grief was still new—a man who wouldn't ask questions or gossip about you later."

Noah was still that way.

"When Keith hired Noah, he was actually choosing the nurse who would be perfect for your first private practice."

She didn't know what to say. She'd believed God had a plan for her life, but she hadn't thought how far ahead God planned. How awesome, that He'd set things in motion that long ago!

Sunday evening was Noah's best night of the week. He and Kendi had their chores done, and he settled into his recliner with a big bowl of buttered popcorn.

Usually, Kendi sat on his lap and shared the popcorn while they took turns watching kid shows and sports, but tonight Kendi wasn't hungry, and she lay on the floor on her tummy, staring listlessly at the TV. It was a show she usually enjoyed.

"How are you doing, Kendi?" he asked as he already had, twice in the last half hour.

"'Kay," she answered as before.

Kids could get sick incredibly fast. He lay down beside her to check her over. She didn't seem to have a fever, a rash or anything other than this lethargy. "Kendi, I think you may need to see the doctor tomorrow and have her take a look at you."

"Tomorrow?" She sat up, miraculously perky. "Yep, I'm kinda sick. I should see the doctor!"

"You think so?"

"I could have low sugar...or blood pressure... or bunions!"

"Ooh, that would be bad," he said, trying to keep a straight face. "Does Harlene have those problems?"

"She does! And it might be catching. I'll go to work with you so Beth can see what I got." Her eyes sparkled with good health—and hope.

"But we always take you to Dr. Marsha." How far would his strong-willed daughter take this?

"Yep, but I think Beth is the goodest doctor."

Automatically he corrected, "Beth is the better doctor."

"I think so, too."

Okay, he didn't have the energy for a grammar lesson. He'd have to let that one slide.

"I'll take the yellow hot pad I made with Harlene, and I'll wear my pink dress, the one with the flowers. Beth really likes it, and I L-O-V-E, love that dress. You got it for me, Daddy."

"Kendra, I think we'll wait a few days and see if your bunions and blood pressure don't improve."

"Nooo, Daddy!"

His child's disappointment hit him like a physical blow. It always did, and all too often, he gave in to whatever she wanted. But sometimes a dad knew best, even if the little love of his life didn't think so.

He stayed firm with Kendra on Monday.

On Tuesday, he had to put his little girl in time-out for incessant begging to see Beth.

On Wednesday she handed him a stack of pictures and sweetly asked him to take them to Beth. All of the pictures were of a lady with short blond hair wearing yellow shoes. He said he would take one.

Of course, Beth loved it. On her lunch hour, she bought Kendi a new set of markers and drawing paper and sent them home with him, along with a note, requesting pictures of flowers and rainbows.

That night, Kendi sat at the counter, using her new markers to draw what she wanted—another picture of Beth. "Daddy, I like having Beth for my friend."

"She's a good person to have as a friend," he answered parentally, but it was true. It was only their second week of working together, but he could see himself working with her a long time—providing he got over the distraction of working in such close quarters with a very cute doc.

"Daddy, I've been thinking."

That was never good. Usually his child blurted out every thought. When she bothered with a setup, she had an agenda. "Whatcha thinkin', Kendi?" he said, steeling himself to be firm.

"I've been thinking I want to have pizza this Friday with my friend, Beth."

Man, she sounded so sweet. He hated what he had to do. "That's not an option, Kendra. What did I tell you last week when you brought this up?"

His daughter's eyes clouded, and her lower lip quivered. "You said it was you and me having pizza, or you would cook those bad beans and rice."

"That's right. And it's the same deal this week."

Quietly, she packed up her markers, closed her drawing pad and slid off the counter stool.

"The mac and cheese is almost ready."

"I don't want any."

She'd never turned down mac and cheese. He

watched her cross the living room and head toward her bedroom. He gave her a few minutes before going to see what she was up to.

It broke his heart. She was packing her little suitcase.

"Whatcha doing, sweetheart?"

"I'm gonna go live with Harlene," his baby said, a catch in her voice.

He knelt and pulled her into his arms. "But what would Daddy do without his little girl?"

She laid her head on his shoulder, wrapped her arms around his neck and broke down, sobbing.

He choked back tears of his own.

A good parent didn't give in to the pressure of his child, but a really good parent listened. Kendi said she wanted to see Beth. She'd said it and said it.

Of all people, he should have understood. He knew what it was like to be around Beth. She lit up a room, just walking into it. His daughter needed that kind of joy, but he'd been so busy worrying about Kendi depending on Beth, that he'd missed the point. Kendi needed what Beth could offer, and she needed it now.

Kendi fidgeted in her chair at Sluggers and checked the door every time it opened, which was often, with customers arriving for take-out orders.

Tony and Barb—Friday night regulars like himself and Kendi—sat at the next table. "Why haven't you ordered your pizza, Kendra?" Tony asked. "Aren't you hungry tonight?"

"We're waiting for somebody very special," Kendi said.

Somebody special was very late. He'd already explained that doctors have emergencies, but if Beth didn't show up, Kendi would be—

"There she is!" Kendi cried, jumping out of her seat before he could stop her and rushing to meet Beth.

Beth knelt down to hug her, putting herself on Kendi's level the way she did with her patients. Kendi threw herself into Beth's arms and held on tight.

"You've got a beautiful wife, Noah," Tony said. "You can sure tell those two are mother and daughter."

His wife, Barb, said, "We haven't seen her before. Does your wife usually work late?"

Barb and Tony were very nice people. He didn't want to embarrass them or make them feel bad. "That's my boss," he answered. "She's a pediatrician, and she's really good with kids. Kendi's crazy about her."

"I can see that!" Tony said.

"My wife passed away a couple of years ago,"

Noah added, though he dreaded the sympathy that was sure to come.

"Oh, I'm so sorry!" Barb exclaimed.

"Not a problem," he assured them, pulling out a chair for Beth as Kendi pointed out the assigned seating.

Beth touched his arm, a way to say hello while she listened intently to Kendi. Beth was a toucher, a hugger, a loving person who reached out to everyone. The little touch on his arm was just a friendly gesture, not anything that should set his heart racing or make him wonder what would happen if it were just the two of them here.

On this warm October night, Beth wore shorts and a T-shirt. The shirt matched the color of her caramel eyes, and her shorts showed off a pair of truly great legs. Her yellow sneakers apparently had the night off. Tan flip-flops took their place.

They placed their order, and Kendi presented Beth with the hot pad she'd made. Beth asked about Harlene, and Kendi gave a full report—bunions, blood pressure, sugar and all.

In the noisy restaurant, Beth had to lean forward to hear Kendra. It put her in a brighter light, and he realized that Beth looked exhausted. She hadn't seemed this tired when they left the office.

He pulled a coin from his pocket. "Kendi, would you like to get your gum ball now?"

"Now?" she said, astonished.

He never allowed the treat until they were through eating, but a guy got creative when he wanted to speak to someone alone.

Kendi took the money quickly and dashed away.

"What happened, Beth?"

"You can tell? I know you seem to read my mind at work, but I thought that was just you being the perfect nurse."

"What happened?" he repeated, wanting to know before Kendi got back.

"I got a call from New York. A patient of mine was killed today."

"Killed?"

"Just before I left there, I sutured a knife wound on the arm of an eleven-year-old boy. He said he got it 'practicing fighting' with his older brother. I don't know if he was practicing again or fighting for real, but he got cut, and whoever did it left him to bleed out."

What could he say? He reached for her hand.

Her fleeting glance said she appreciated the comforting gesture. "The boy, Stevie, asked me out on a date." She smiled, but tears welled in her eyes. "I told him I'd go if he took me to church. He said he'd think about it. I hope he went anyway."

"He probably did," Noah said, mostly to make her to feel better.

"I'd like to believe that."

Her wistful look went straight to his heart.

"I feel so responsible. I turned him over to social services, but if I'd stayed in New York, this might not have happened."

She was smarter than that. She was just hurting. "Knowing you, I expect you prayed about leaving."

She nodded.

"Did you feel it was the right thing to do?"

"Very much so."

"Then why second-guess yourself now?"

The question seemed to catch Beth by surprise. "Good point. I'm glad one of us remembered that God has a plan for our lives," she said, withdrawing her hand.

Kendra was on her way back. "I didn't get a yellow one," she said sorrowfully, slumping into her chair.

"But any color is better than no gum ball at all, right?" he said, with a warning look.

"Right!" She sat up straight and put on a happy face even if it wasn't genuine.

He leaned toward her and murmured, "Good job."

That made her smile for real.

Kendi introduced Beth to Tony and Barb, and they all chatted until their pizza was served.

"Is it your turn to pray or mine?" Kendi asked Beth.

"Yours," Beth said, bowing her head.

It was so noisy in the restaurant, and Kendi prayed so softly, that he couldn't hear what she said, but he heard her at every other meal and knew she would be praying for a long list of people plus current events. Somewhere, she'd gotten the idea that long prayers were best, despite the fact that the food could get cold before she finished.

He felt like a hypocrite, encouraging Kendi to believe in her mother's faith when he didn't anymore, but it had been important to Merrilee, and she would have wanted this.

He sneaked a peak at Beth. Her smile tilted the corners of her mouth. Man, he loved that smile.

When Kendi was through, Beth said, "That was a wonderful prayer, Kendra."

Kendi nodded, not taking the comment as a compliment, but a statement of truth. "That's 'cause I get so much practice."

"That's right," Beth said knowingly. "You're the official pray-er at your house."

"Yep. Praying is my job. Cutting things, like my pizza, is Daddy's job."

He slid pieces onto her plate. "Careful, Kendi. It's still hot."

"He's a really good dad, isn't he?" Beth said.

Kendi nodded so emphatically, he hoped she wouldn't hurt herself. His baby didn't do anything halfway.

"And Daddy's a really good boyfriend," she said.

"Kendra!" He choked on his diet cola.

"What makes him a good boyfriend?" Beth asked, egging his daughter on.

There would be payback for that.

"If you want to go to the park, he'll take you. He'll push you if you want to swing, and he fixes really good food, like hot dogs and macaroni and cheese. He can make brownies out of a box and dee-licious popcorn."

"With butter?"

"Oh, yeah! Lots of butter!"

"Wow!" Beth exclaimed. "Your dad *is* a good boyfriend."

"I know," Kendi agreed, beaming at him.

That smile was what he lived for.

"Kendi, remember that we take turns talking," he said parentally. "Ask Beth something about herself."

"Okay, but I have to think of something." She nibbled on her pizza, working around a loose tooth. "I know!"

Anything was better than his merit as a boyfriend.

"Beth, do you have a boyfriend?"

He choked again.

"Are you all right, Noah?" Beth asked, her eyes laughing at him. "Need any help from the doctor?"

He waved off the help and looked around for a hole to crawl in.

"*Do* you have a boyfriend, Beth?" his daughter asked again, relentless as only she could be.

"Ask her something else, Kendra," he said firmly.

"Kendra, I have a question for you," Beth said. "Do *you* have a boyfriend?"

By the time Kendi finished comparing William and Justin to the other male prospects at Loma Verde Elementary, she was totally distracted. Beth kept her talking—about the kids' program at church, about her toy animals and the names of her dolls—and soon the meal was over.

He was impressed. Beth had made this a wonderful time for Kendi, and he'd been enjoying himself so much he hadn't noticed when Barb and Tony left.

He boxed their leftovers in two containers—one for Beth, one for himself and Kendi. They had plenty. He'd been so nervous, wondering what his little girl would say next, he hadn't eaten much. Beth had eaten almost nothing, though she'd professed to love pizza, and he wondered if she was too upset about that poor kid in New York.

"What are you two doing tomorrow?" Beth asked as they stood and he left tip money on the table.

"Me and daddy go bike-riding every Saturday morning," Kendi answered. "Only just me rides. Daddy runs."

"Only just *I* ride," he corrected automatically.

"Daddy, you never ride. You always run."

"I wondered what Daddy did to work out," Beth said, giving him an approving nod.

"Mostly Daddy cleans and does laundry," he said dryly, pretending he didn't notice she was checking him out.

"The black T-shirt and tan shorts—it's a good look for you," she said, checking him out, head to toe. "But I don't think you get those particular muscles doing laundry. You lift weights, right?"

"If you call lifting Kendra, weights."

"Daddy whirls me around," Kendi said. "And I'm the only-est kid as big as me who rides on Daddy's shoulders."

"That must have been when you were little. Your daddy looks strong, but he couldn't carry a second-grader who's just turned seven around on his shoulders," she said, a challenge in her eyes.

"Yes, he can." Kendi lifted her arms up to him, ready to be lifted so she could prove her claim.

He took her hands, but just to hold them. "The shoulder ride is a move reserved for crowded places, Kendi, so you can get a better view or so you won't get lost."

"Right. I didn't think you could do it," Beth teased.

For a half a second, he considered proving her wrong, but that was the kind of thing a kid did to show off for a very cute girl. He was a man with a boatload of responsibility.

Outside, they walked to her car and talked a bit. None of them seemed eager to go home, particularly Kendi who held Beth's hand as if she might never have the chance again.

"Beth, would you like to go bike-riding with us tomorrow?" Kendi asked, dodging his eyes. She knew better than to issue an invitation without checking with him first.

"Really?" Beth seemed pleased. "If it's okay with your daddy…." She looked at him hopefully.

How would Kendi ever learn if he gave in all the time? But how could he say no, with both of them looking at him so hopefully?

"We leave early," he said, "about eight, from our house." Having Beth along would start the day with an extra punch of joy.

Beth grimaced and said, "Could we go a little later. I promised to have breakfast with my grandfather tomorrow."

He thought of their Saturday schedule and braced himself for his daughter's reaction. "Another time we could go later, but not tomorrow."

"Daddy!" Kendi was horrified, as expected.

"I'm sorry, puddin', but tomorrow is Harlene's day."

"But, Daddy…."

"She needs to have her hair done. We're going to help her buy groceries, get her medicine, lots of things—and we're taking her out to eat. Remember?"

"But that was before…." She stopped on his silencing look. Turning to Beth, she said, "We gotta take care of Harlene, 'cause we're her fam'ly."

Beth looked at him as if to say, "What a kid!"

He appreciated her opinion more than she would imagine.

Chapter Eleven

Beth produced a coin and said, "Kendra, why don't you go try for a yellow gum ball again?"

His daughter hesitated, torn between staying another minute with Beth and going for the prize.

"Go for it, Kendi," he said.

That was the boost she needed. Did Beth have something she wanted to say privately?

"Noah, I know Kendra put you on the spot again. I had a genuine reason I couldn't go with you two in the morning, but what do we do when she includes me in your plans another time? You shouldn't have to be the bad dad, and I can't be less than truthful with her."

"You're right, but it feels wrong, letting Kendi take over your life. I want her to have what you can give, but give her an inch, and she'll take a mile. She'll want to hang out with you all the time."

"She will, won't she?"

Their shared smile made him feel as if they were a couple.

"Children are like that," she said with an understanding sigh. "They stay as close as your shadow, then, in their teen years, they don't want to be seen with you at all. I would love to hang out with Kendra and you!"

"Really?" With all the people she knew in L.A., she wanted to be with them? Did she love kids that much?

"You must be wondering what will happen to my friendship with Kendra as my friendship with you changes. Friendships evolve. You might get sick of seeing me all day plus after hours. Anything could happen."

It was great that Beth was thinking ahead.

"As Kendra's dad, you need to know that I'm signing on to be her friend, regardless of what happens with us."

"And you're cool with that? You would be Kendi's friend even if we weren't friends?"

She nodded. "I would be if you allowed it."

"And I don't have to worry about Kendi taking too much of your time?"

"No! Do I have to worry that you'll think I'm overstepping your parental authority if I suggest something I think she will enjoy?"

"Not a bit."

"Promise?" She offered her hand.

"Promise," he said, shaking on the deal.

His daughter came back, holding a pink gum ball in her hand. "I didn't get yellow, but pink is next best," she said with a decent attitude.

"Would you two like to have dessert at my house?" Beth offered, glancing at him as if to say this was a test of their new agreement. "I have an animated video."

Kendi couldn't have been more thrilled by a box full of yellow gum balls. "Don't say 'no,' Daddy," she said, as if she feared he might.

"You'll probably fall asleep, Kendi."

"I can stay awake."

"Or you can sleep over," Beth said. "Maybe Daddy would enjoy a run by himself in the morning."

Daddy would love that. "Didn't you say you were having breakfast with your grandfather?"

"Yes, but Grandpa would love to have Kendra come, too. Maybe you and Harlene could do a few errands while Kendra and I do some girl stuff. Kendra hasn't seen our Noah's Ark theme yet. We could meet you at the clinic about noon."

His daughter looked at him with stars in her eyes. "Could we do that, Daddy?"

He felt a little starry-eyed himself. Beth had

just rearranged their lives, yet the load of responsibility he carried like a knapsack full of stones seemed lighter.

From her kitchen cupboard, Beth chose three wide-mouthed goblets that she'd bought for this particular dessert. She placed scoops of raspberry sherbet in the goblets and topped them with freshly cut bananas, strawberries, nectarines and pineapple.

Her cohostess Kendra stuck chocolate-filled wafers into the sherbet and served it with flair to her daddy.

The three of them had shared breakfast out here on the balcony, but tonight, recessed lighting added to the glow of candles around the room. A warm breeze ruffled the feathery fronds of palm trees as tall as her third-floor balcony.

"This looks too pretty to eat," Noah said.

"I don't cook," Beth confessed, bringing the other servings to the table, "so I go for points on presentation."

"Daddy can cook," Kendra said, spooning banana into her mouth. "And he only makes you eat a little food that's good for you before you get the stuff you like."

"It's a perfect night, isn't it?" Noah said, glancing around the balcony as if he hadn't seen it before.

Beth hid a smile. She loved Kendra's PR campaign to present Noah as Boyfriend of the Year, but, if she were him, it would be hard to take.

"You could live out here, it's so big," he said.

"My whole apartment in New York was smaller," she said, helping him move the subject to an impersonal topic. "I love being out here."

"In California or on the balcony?" he teased.

"Both! But the balcony is my favorite place. I love the warm breeze. Kendra, in New York, right now, the kids are probably wearing jackets to school."

"Yep, 'cause it's autumn. I learned it at school. You know what happened at school today? Baylee wanted to be a door holder, and she cutted me." Kendra's big lavender-blue eyes said that was a most grievous offense. "Me and Brooke were supposed to be door holders. You are not supposed to cut people. Baylee had to go to the back of the line."

Beth nodded, sympathetically. Noah's eyes glazed over, as if he'd heard this before.

"I like to be first," Kendra continued, "but I can't or no one will like me."

Noah had done his job, or his daughter wouldn't have that kind of insight.

"I like to play with Baylee and Brooke. They're twins! I wish I was a twin."

"Beth, did you say you had a video we could watch?" Noah said, sliding back from the table and taking their dishes to the kitchen.

She put the video in, and Kendra orchestrated the seating arrangement, putting them all on the sofa, with herself in the middle.

Ten minutes into the animated movie, she snuggled into Beth's arms as if she belonged there.

Beth looked at Noah. Was he as surprised as she was?

He gestured for her to take another look.

His child was fast asleep.

"You called that one," she said, shutting off the kiddie flick. "I wish I could do that."

"She's always been that way. Her mother used to say it was God's gift to a deserving parent. I worked the night shift and didn't realize what Merrilee meant until I took care of Kendi by myself."

"It's a big job, being a single parent. Can I ask you something?"

One corner of his mouth lifted in that lopsided smile that got to her every time. He shifted so he could face her and rested his arm across the top of the sofa. "Since you've given me time off from Kendi care, you can ask anything."

Relaxed this way, he was more appealing than ever. Fluttery butterflies in her stomach said so, too.

"What do you want to know?" he prompted.

"About what?" For some reason she couldn't seem to focus.

"You had a question?"

She had many questions. Am I falling for you? Are you feeling what I am? "How did you meet Kendra's mother, Noah?" she asked. That put her brain back on track.

"I met Merrilee at a theme park where we both worked. She was eighteen, fresh out of high school. I was twenty-one and taking junior college courses. Don't laugh, but I thought I wanted to be a doctor."

"What's funny about that? I can see you as a doctor."

He shrugged and gave her one of his lopsided smiles. "I traded that idea for a family."

"Can't you have both?"

"Let's say, *I* couldn't. Three years before I met Merrilee, I'd aged out of the foster-care system. I'd learned how to take care of myself, but Merrilee had just aged out and was still finding her way. We had a lot in common. Both of us had been unadoptable. We'd been moved from place to place. Neither of us had anybody."

It was amazing how unemotionally Noah related the bare facts. His life and Merrilee's would have been filled with trauma, heartache and loneliness.

"Merrilee needed me—the first person who ever had…" His voice cracked a little on that. "I loved having someone to take care of."

He didn't mention needing Merrilee. Kids raised like Noah learned to deny need, even to themselves. Beth knew that as well as she knew the best meds to prescribe for her patients. "God brought you two together, didn't He?"

"That's what Merrilee said."

Before Beth was a Christian, she wouldn't have considered that possibility, but, now, she believed it. "When did you know you were in love?"

"When?" He closed his eyes, as if he were trying to remember. "I think it was when Merrilee asked me to marry her. I was such a chicken, I would never have asked her."

"Did you say yes?"

"Oh, yeah! We were married the next week. I was afraid she would change her mind."

She wouldn't have. If a woman had Noah's love, she would be his forever.

"When Merrilee became pregnant, I switched to the nursing program. I liked it. We did okay."

"I'd say you did a lot better than okay. The two of you raised a wonderful daughter."

His smile faded, and he looked at her with concern. "Beth, you see how Kendi can talk me into almost anything. I want her to grow up to be confident and sure of herself, but not headstrong or self-centered. You're an expert on kids. Tell me the truth. Do I need to toughen up?"

"You want me to tell you the truth?"

"Even if it hurts."

"Then, here's what I have to say. Ready?"

He nodded. A muscle twitched in his jaw.

"The truth is…I wish I'd had a dad like you."

It was almost noon when Noah drove past the BMC physicians' parking lot, but Beth's car was already there. He had dropped Harlene off at the salon for her hair appointment early, yet Beth and Kendi had beaten him here. It was a small thing, but he would have liked to be with Kendi when she caught her first glimpse of the lobby.

He ran to the door nearest the employee parking lot, wondering if he could get to the office faster if he took the elevator or ran up the stairs three at a time?

"Hi, Daddy!" his baby exclaimed as he yanked open the door. She jumped up from the stairs where she had been sitting with Beth and lifted her arms for their daddy-daughter kiss.

"You were waiting for me?"

"Yep, Beth said we couldn't see the ark without Noah," she said, giggling at the little joke.

Beth's eyes swept the length of him and came

back to rest on Kendi, holding him tight. She'd looked just like that when she'd said she wished she'd had a dad like him. He felt a tug on his heart.

"I don't know about you two," Beth said, "but I'm taking the elevator. Anybody coming with me?"

"Me!" Kendi volunteered, sliding out of his arms.

"How about you, Daddy?" Beth teased, challenge in her caramel-colored eyes. "Do you want to take the stairs and try to beat us?"

He'd never been one to resist a challenge, but he'd had enough of being alone. It felt too good, being with Kendi and Beth…though he would like it better if Beth would stop calling him Daddy.

In the elevator, Kendi claimed the privilege of pushing the third-floor button. That gave him a chance to touch Beth's arm and say, "Thanks for waiting for me."

She just smiled.

"Daddy, did you see my new outfit?" Kendi preened, showing off the front and back of a yellow top and matching skirt, or maybe it was what they called a skort. She pulled the front flap aside, and shorts were underneath.

"We went shopping," Beth said, though he could see that for himself.

"You look so cute, Kendi!" he said, approving the new look which included her hair brushed back from her face and secured with a cluster of curly bright ribbons.

"Daddy looks pretty cute himself," Beth said, taking in his white shorts and yellow T-shirt.

"I gave that shirt to Daddy for his birthday," Kendi said, accepting the compliment. She pointed to Noah's and Beth's yellow T-shirts and white shorts. "You're twins! Daddy, you match Beth!"

"Not really," he said, pretending this was not supremely embarrassing. "I don't have the yellow shoes."

"When's your birthday?" Beth asked. "I'll get you a pair of yellow leather Nikes. They do custom orders."

That was all he needed, yellow sneakers of his own.

"We're the yellow family," Kendi said happily.

"What do you think, Noah?" Beth said with a wry smile. "Do we look like tourists, heading for a theme park?"

He looked from his outfit to hers and just shook his head. This was not a manly moment.

"We're go-ing to see No-ah's ark," Kendi sang, taking his hand and Beth's as if she were as thrilled with the journey as the destination.

That changed when the lobby came into view.

"Oh!" Kendi was as speechless as he'd been the first time he'd seen Beth's ark.

"That's a *big* promise rainbow!" she exclaimed.

Beth looked at him and whispered, "A promise rainbow?"

He nodded and whispered back, "Later."

Kendi had to sit in each little animal chair, admire each little fishie and check out the Noah's ark mural in detail. Beth stood beside him, watching Kendi explore, just like a proud parent herself.

Inside the office, Beth flipped on the exam room lights, and Kendi went from room to room, laughing at the silly murals. Beth opened a hat cabinet and invited Kendi to try them all.

He sat on the exam table and patted the spot beside him, inviting Beth to join him for the style show.

Beth leaned close and asked softly, "Why did she call it a promise rainbow?"

Noah kept his voice low. "She heard the Noah story at church a couple of years ago. I imagine they told it like the Bible says—the rainbow was God's promise not to destroy the earth by a flood again, but Kendi put it in the context of her own life. To her, a rainbow is God's promise that everything will turn out okay. I haven't had the heart to tell her any different."

Beth smiled at Kendra and said quietly, "Her theology isn't off much. If God can make a rainbow, He can make everything turn out okay."

He wouldn't argue, but how could she be that sure?

Beth sat in the church sanctuary, waiting for her brother and Meg. A well-trained orchestra played beautiful preservice music. The seats were padded with velvety cushions, and lush green plants were everywhere.

It was quite a contrast from Beth's store-front church near Manhattan Free Clinic, but the presence of the Lord was real in both places.

Meg and Ry slid into the seats beside her. Meg started to hug her, but she stopped and did a double-take.

"You're wearing makeup!" she said. Her eyes swept Beth from top to bottom. "And earrings! And heels! I can't believe it."

Neither could Beth. The makeup felt heavy, the earrings pinched and the shoes were pure torture.

"Nice dress, sis," Ry murmured, leaning over to give Beth a kiss. "What's the occasion?"

"She's met someone," Meg said with smug certainty.

"Good for you, sis! It's about time."

"Tell me about him." Meg nudged Beth's shoulder, the way good friends do.

"There is no him," Beth said, nudging her back. She wished that weren't true, but it was. For the first time since Luke, she *was* interested in a man, but Noah wasn't interested in her.

"You can tell me later," Meg said, patting her arm as the worship service began.

What was there to tell? That she was falling for a great guy who didn't see her as more than a friend of the family? Yesterday, she'd joined Noah, Kendra and Harlene after they'd left the clinic. She'd been as tingly aware of him as a teenager with a crush, but Noah seemed more aware of Harlene. Of course, it had been Harlene's day, and the measure of a good man was how he treated his mother—or a precious older woman like Harlene.

Beth didn't know the first song, but everyone else seemed to. Her brother sang with a boldness that tore at her heart. When Ry and Meg had been her childhood buddies, she'd never imagined the three of them would be here like this.

Across the aisle and down a few rows, Meg's brother, Pete, sat with his wife, Sunny. During the offertory, Pete slipped his arm around Sunny and bent his head near hers. They made an attractive couple, with his ebony hair and her coppery curls.

To the left of Beth and up one row, her cousin Collin sat with his fiancée, Glenda. In three weeks, they would be married in the garden of this church. Beth was so proud of Ry for leading them to the Lord. If he weren't studying to be a doctor, he could have been a preacher. He and Meg sat shoulder to shoulder, her hand in his, the two of them more in love than ever.

Beth looked around, and it seemed as if she saw couples everywhere—retirees, middle-aged people, young parents, even teenagers—all of them sitting two by two. She'd never complained about being single the way some women do, but suddenly, the longing to have a man of her own hit like a pang of hunger that wouldn't be ignored.

Lord, remember when I said I wasn't desperate? I must have been in denial. If what I'm feeling is the biological-clock thing common to women my age, that's okay. I'll understand. If it's something worse, like self-pity or depression, that's not fine at all!

Am I over-thinking this?

Simple faith is what You want. Uneasiness can be Your way of getting us ready for the next thing in Your plan. Could it be that You're preparing me to trust one man again?

Who do You have in mind?

She let it rest while she sang the worship songs, but during the announcements, her mind wandered.

Once, she'd loved Luke Jordahl, and he was still drop-dead gorgeous. He'd said he'd changed, but she hadn't seen it. If he knew the Lord, Luke could be a man worthy of loving…just not by her…not without a major sign from God.

Zack Hemmingway was interested in her, and she liked him a lot. He reminded her so much of her dad—both of them brilliant specialists who lived for their work. She didn't have much to go on, but she thought there was a lonely guy beneath Zack's confident appearance, and she wanted to get to know him better. Unfortunately, there didn't seem to be any special chemistry between them.

She'd missed part of the sermon, but the title on the big overhead screen said, Surrender to the Possibilities.

The pastor was about her age and seemed like a great guy with a cool sense of humor. She leaned toward Meg and whispered, "Is the pastor married?"

Meg nodded.

"Is his wife here?"

Meg pointed out a petite redhead.

The woman looked nice. She and the pastor made another great couple.

"In the Bible, God used people in unexpected ways," said Pastor Already-Taken. He gave a bunch of examples—Jonah, Moses, Peter, Paul—and Beth wrote on her sermon outline page, "When you act from fear, when you make snap judgments, when you shut people out, you may be shutting the door on God's plan for your life."

The door to her relationship with Noah was more like a swinging door. It ought to stay shut because office romances were a bad idea, but if she took the sermon to heart, shouldn't she surrender to the possibilities?

Chapter Twelve

Hot October sun beat down on Noah's SUV as he waited patiently for Harlene to straggle out of church. She didn't get to socialize often, so he didn't mind. Like a good girl, Kendi waited just as patiently in the back seat.

"Daddy, here's something for you to read." She handed him a paper that said the church was having a pre-Thanksgiving celebration in three weeks. A different event was scheduled for each night of the week. Monday through Wednesday were ethnic events; Thursday was a Mother-Daughter Tea and Friday was a Father-Son Game Night.

"Noah, did Kendra give you the celebration handout?" Harlene asked, opening the door and pulling herself into the front passenger seat. The exertion made her short of breath, and, despite the chilled air pouring from the air conditioner, she fanned herself with a church bulletin.

"Got it right here," he answered, waving the paper.

"Excellent. Kendra, when your teacher told you about all the parties, were they like what we talked about?" Harlene asked as Noah pulled the SUV into traffic.

"Yep. I'm going to the Mother-Daughter Tea. Only they don't make you drink tea. They have lemonade."

"Did Harlene offer to take you, Kendi, or did you ask her nicely?" Noah hoped she'd remembered her manners.

In the rearview mirror, he saw Kendi shake her head. "Nope. Harlene isn't going to take me."

"You're not?" he asked Harlene, frowning.

"No. Mary Jane, Carole and Jan are taking me to one of the ethnic nights. We haven't decided which one."

"Can't a person go to more than one event?" He couldn't believe Harlene would let Kendi down.

"Yes, but Kendra plans to ask Beth to take her."

"You've talked about this? We just got the handout."

"Oh, I've known for a while. After meeting Beth Brennan yesterday, I approve of Kendra's choice."

Who wouldn't? It was always more fun when she was around, but could a little girl like Kendi understand that Beth was just their friend? How long would she be content with Beth as a stand-in mom, and not the real thing?

"Kendi, let's you and me go to the fiesta on Monday night of the celebration week," he said. "You love tacos."

"'Kay."

Good. That was settled.

"But I'm still going to the Mother-Daughter Tea."

He should have known he couldn't change her mind.

As soon as they got home, Kendi wanted to call Beth, but he reminded her that Beth was having brunch with her uncle and aunt. Kendi didn't like that one bit, and, truthfully, Noah wasn't crazy about it either.

Beth hadn't said, but he figured Zack Hemmingway would be there, too. Vanessa had reported that the two of them were a hot topic on the BMC grapevine. Dr. Al Brennan was supposedly pushing the romance.

If Beth was seeing Zack, she didn't talk about it, though who Beth dated wasn't any of Noah's business. His only concern was the little blond girl sitting in her room, drawing pictures of a blond lady while she fretted the minutes away, waiting for her chance to call Beth.

Until Beth came into their lives, Noah hadn't noticed how intent Kendi was on connecting with a new mother. He hadn't reached that stage of readiness, but this Mother-Daughter Tea had him convinced. He ought to get out there and get to know some mommy candidates.

Women had hinted of their availability. Now, if he could only remember who some of them were.

Glenda's sister, Marissa, taught Kendi to swim. She had a teenage son and was a little older than Noah, but not much. Kendi would like a big brother.

William's mother was an absolute knockout, but William was an absolute brat, so they wouldn't go there. Dr. Marsha Clayton's nurse, Kris Young, was a terrific person who had a lot in common with him, and Kendi liked her a lot.

Their neighbor, Stephanie, made great cookies and had two kids for Kendi to play with. And then there was Merrilee's best friend, JoEllyn, who'd been there for them, especially the first few months after the funeral.

He wrote the names down and called for Kendi to join him in his big recliner. She snuggled in, laying her head on his chest, and would probably go to sleep if his list of mommy candidates didn't interest her.

"Kendi, about the Mother-Daughter Tea…if Beth can't go for some reason, I have a list of very nice ladies who I think would like to take you. I'll read their names, and you tell me which one is your favorite. Okay?"

"Beth *can* go, Daddy. She'll want to take me."

"But you haven't asked her yet, puddin'. This is a backup plan."

She buried her head and wouldn't look at his list.

Ignoring the attitude, he named off the choices. "So, who's the winner, sweetheart? Who would you like to have take you to the Mother-Daughter Tea?"

Kendi looked at him with serious blue-violet eyes. "Beth. Just Beth."

"And if she can't go…."

"I don't wanna go."

Beth parked the VW between its pricey neighbors in the BMC physicians' lot and gathered gift bags and a floral arrangement from the back seat, just as she had two weeks ago. The flowers were in a darling elephant pitcher that Meg had shared from her jungle decor. They would by-pass the lobby and go straight to her office, adding to the Noah's Ark theme she'd started in there.

For Vanessa, she had bags of candy to refill the

kangaroo dish. For Mona, who definitely loved chocolate, Beth had a half pound of the best chocolate truffles money could buy. For Noah, she'd shopped a little harder for the perfect gift.

She hadn't known what to give him until Kendra had called and invited her to the Mother-Daughter Tea. Beth had felt such pleasure, accepting. Then Noah had stolen her joy of the moment, saying she shouldn't feel obligated to take Kendra to the party, and it was okay to tell Kendra no. He didn't want to take advantage of Beth's kindness.

It sounded to her as if he were backpedaling from their new friendship. Even if he was thinking of how attached she and Kendi were becoming, couldn't he trust that she wouldn't hurt a child? If he thought she wouldn't keep her promise to be a friend whom Kendra could count on, he could go fly a kite.

He had a brand-new one. She'd found it when they were shopping with Harlene Saturday afternoon. His kite was a beautiful promise-rainbow kite that would look glorious flying high in the sky. She'd bought it with the intention of taking Kendra kite-flying herself.

Trying to see things from his viewpoint, Beth could understand that Noah might be leery of how fast their friendship had taken off. It did send up a red flag that Kendra would ask her to be a mother substitute after a two-week acquaintance, but kids made up their minds fast. They recognized who was a phoney and who loved them for real.

Maybe if Beth were extremely busy with children of her own, she wouldn't have had the time to reach out to Kendra. As it was, Beth thought the Lord had placed her in Kendra's life when the little girl really needed her and when Beth was lonely for someone to love.

She entered the office suite from her private office, donned her lab coat and left the gifts on her desk where they could stay until her little thank-you presentation at the end of the day. On her way to the front office, she saw that all three exam rooms were occupied, but she'd admitted a patient to the hospital this morning and was running a little late.

"Good morning!" Vanessa exclaimed with her usual cheerful smile. "You have one message from the lab, and Dr. Al Brennan's receptionist called to say you left your sunglasses at his house. Dr. Hemmingway will drop them off this morning."

"Good morning, Beth," Noah said, behind her.

Even if he hadn't spoken, she would have known he was there from the faint scent he wore.

She turned, their eyes met and her knees seemed to buckle. She reached for the counter before she literally fell for the guy.

"Good morning, Noah." She sounded normal, not like a woman down for the count. "Which patient is first?"

"The Logan twins—Mariah and Makenzie—in Room Three."

"The Logans…are they the ones you were concerned about cancelling on my second day?"

His eyes flared with anger. "I called their mother. Teri said they *didn't* cancel. Mona told them *you* had to."

A shiver went through Beth. Was Mona behind those other cancellations as well?

Lord, what do I do about Mona? Am I wrong to think she'll change if I keep showing her Your love?

In the office of Dr. J. T. Brennan, Sr., Noah sat on the edge of a leather couch, dreading the moment Beth would walk in and see him with her grandfather. Since Mona's shenanigans hadn't pushed Beth's buttons, he hoped Beth wouldn't be mad at him…but anyone else would be.

Her grandfather sat in a high-backed chair, his white hair a stark contrast to the dark upholstery. His age-worn face was grim, but determined.

Noah understood. He was as fiercely protective of Kendi as the chief was of Beth.

Beth joined them and did a double-take when she saw he was here, but her smile seemed even brighter.

That was a good sign.

"Noah, what are you doing here?" she asked pleasantly, greeting her grandfather with a hug.

"I invited him," her grandfather said. His voice, unsteady with age, still held authority. Before he'd founded Brennan Medical Clinic, he'd been chief of staff at Cedar Hills Hospital. That was before Noah's time there, but J. T. Brennan was a legend. "Thank you both for giving up your lunch time. In a few minutes, we'll raid my refrigerator and have something here."

"Wait 'til you see what Grandpa squirrels away in his fridge," Beth said, sitting beside Noah on the couch. "It's better than the clinic cafeteria."

The chief cleared his throat, signaling that the pleasantries were over. "Beth, when you were in New York, I promised that you could run your office any way you liked, and I've done that, haven't I?"

"You have! You've been amazing, Grandpa."

"Thank you, darling. I have complete confidence in your ability to do a great job—as Keith did when he chose you as his replacement. After you agreed to come back, a problem arose that concerned us deeply. You may take exception to the way we decided to solve that problem, but, keep in mind, we did what we thought we had to do."

Beth's smile faded, and her eyes narrowed. It wasn't a look Noah had seen before.

"The reason Noah is here is because he's been my eyes and ears in your office since—"

"Your *what?*" She stood to her feet, instantly angry.

Noah felt a jolt of adrenaline. He hadn't expected her to get that mad that fast.

"You had Noah reporting to you?" She looked at the two of them in shocked disgust.

"He didn't want to, and I hated to ask him, but someone had to watch Mona."

"*I* could have watched Mona. I've *been* watching Mona."

"Listen to reason, darling. You weren't here when Keith knocked the pins from beneath the woman's feet. She thought he was going on a fishing trip, not leaving forever. You weren't here when we offered her a retirement package, and she not only refused it, she threatened to sue us for age discrimination if we let her go. You didn't hear the wild accusations she made to anyone who would listen. Keith said we'd better take her wild fury seriously."

"You could have told me," Beth argued, her voice cold.

"If you'll recall, I did say you should let Mona go. I didn't give you all the pertinent facts, but I told you she was impossible to handle. You were determined to win her over. I had to let you try."

"*Let* me?" she repeated.

Ooh, bad choice of words. Noah's heart went out to the chief.

"I wanted you to have the opportunity to do things *your* way—about everything," the chief rephrased smoothly, making a great comeback. "Now that we have the evidence to let Mona go, she must be fired."

"Evidence?" Beth repeated, her lip curled in disgust.

"Yes, evidence—proof of wrongdoing. We have it, and I'm going to let Mona go today."

"Not unless you want me to go, too," Beth said, digging in her heels.

"What?" The chief's white brows drew together.

Noah felt sick to his stomach. He'd hoped Beth wouldn't react this way.

"You can't keep me out of the loop and expect me to go along with your plans. It's either my office, or it's not. If it is my office, then I have a say in who goes and who stays."

"But, darling, Mona has deliberately sabotaged

your credibility, day after day. Everyone knows it. Think of the clinic's reputation if you won't think of your own."

"Beth, Mona isn't going to stop until she's gotten rid of you." Noah jumped in to help the chief make his case.

"Would you care to share how you know that?" she asked, sarcasm dripping from each word. "Or would the two of you prefer to continue treating me like a child?"

"Nobody's doing that, Beth!" her grandfather protested.

"Then, talk to me about the evidence. I'd like to think you're not ending Mona's employment based on rumors and gossip."

"Of course we're not! But I'd think you would care about the rumors and gossip that come from Mona. They're about you and your family!" The chief pounded the arm of his chair in frustration.

"I don't feel as if I've suffered from anything that's been said. People have been unbelievably nice."

"It's not all about you, Beth. Tell her, Noah."

He really didn't want to do this, but she had to know. "I've tracked down lab reports that didn't show up—more than once. I've corrected false documentation that Mona recorded. I've double-checked written med dosages and kept a constant vigil. Vanessa has watched Mona like a hawk. We know what she's like, Beth. These cancellations are only the tip of the iceberg."

"You did all that without telling me?" she asked, frustration in her eyes.

"I'm sorry, but what were we to think? On your second day here, Mona deliberately misled you so you would be late, and you just blew it off. You knew about Mona telling Stacee Drezek that Dr. Crabtree was coming back! How crazy was that? And what did you do? You said you were going to pray about it."

"I believe in the power of prayer."

"I told you we had strange cancellations, but you didn't question them. I tracked down the reason and discovered Mona had been cancelling your patients! If I had come to you with every suspicion, or let you know how hard Vanessa and I worked to keep a serious mistake from happening, I would have looked as negative and hard to get along with as Mona. And would you have done anything about it but pray?"

Stoically, she'd listened, her arms folded. When he finished, she began pacing the room.

The chief sent him a look that said to be patient. Noah hadn't planned on anything else.

When she stopped in front of him, he could see

that she'd made a decision and knew what she wanted. He only hoped it wasn't his resignation.

"First, let me apologize, Noah." Her clipped professional cadence was so unlike the tender, happy lilt their patients knew. "I'm embarrassed that you and Vanessa had to work under conditions like that."

He took a deep breath. So far, so good.

"Second, I wish I'd given you reason to share your concerns with me, not my grandfather."

"He was following my orders, Beth," her grandfather said quietly. "I insisted upon it."

Fleeting expressions crossed her face. Rage and regret, Noah recognized, but there were others.

"Is Noah still under your orders?"

The chief's lips thinned. She had him in a corner, and Noah felt sorry for the man. When a father—or a grandfather—spent a lifetime loving and protecting his family, it wasn't easy to back off.

"Are you saying you know how you want to take care of this situation?" the chief asked, his eyes steady on hers.

"I am. From now on, Noah brings my office problems to me, not you. Agreed?"

"Agreed." Even though he was in the hot seat, a faint smile hovered on the chief's lips.

It looked like respect and pride to Noah. A man

would feel that when his adult child insisted on standing on her own two feet.

"I want you both to know that I *get* it," she said, glancing from the chief to himself. "I understand that we have a problem, and it can't go unchecked. I do believe in the power of prayer—"

That shot was directed at him.

"But you have my promise that I won't put my patients or any of you in jeopardy. Mona does not go today, but if there's another incident, I'll clear out her desk myself."

For all her fierce determination, Beth looked as if she were hurting inside. This had been a humbling experience for her, and he ached to do something that would make her feel better.

"Beth," he said, putting aside his own doubt, "how do you know that your prayers weren't answered?"

She gave him a quizzical look.

"Well, you prayed, and your grandfather asked me to help. Maybe God directed that. I found out what Mona was up to, and you're in a better position to effect change than you were. Maybe this *is* God's answer to your prayer."

Beth didn't stick around to have lunch with her grandfather. She'd just wanted to get in her car, drive with the top down, let the wind blow through her hair and forget about feeling like a failure.

She'd let her grandfather down. She'd let Noah and Vanessa down. And for what? Just so she could follow her single-minded idealism? She did believe in the power of prayer, but it took time to help someone as deeply damaged as Mona. Kindness and love was the way to bring people to Christ, but in focusing on Mona, she'd left Vanessa and Noah out of the equation.

That was such a big front she'd put on back there in Grandpa's office, saying she knew what had to be done. Generally speaking, she did know, but the specifics certainly rattled around in her mind.

She had to have a talk with Mona, and that talk would happen today, but what should she say? "The game's over, Mona. Shape up or ship out?"

That was the message, wasn't it? What a luxury, to be that blunt.

She left the freeway at the next exit and looped around to head back toward the clinic.

Lord, I need Your wisdom...Your direction. What do I do about Mona? What is honest, real and kind? Is there a way to draw the line and show Your love?

And, Lord, what do I do about Noah? He must

not think much of me if he could go behind my back, but, if he could do that, I'm not so sure I think much of him.

It wasn't her imagination. Noah would not meet her eyes, and he hadn't since their noon meeting with Grandpa. She missed their easy give and take, especially after the closeness they'd shared Friday night and on Saturday with Harlene and Kendra.

Even Vanessa seemed subdued, and Mona wasn't as hateful as usual. Maybe they were all reacting to her own attitude. Certainly, it was one they hadn't seen before.

She'd become the vigilant one. She made a point of never leaving Mona alone with a patient or parent any longer than she had to, even if it meant she had to do callbacks at less convenient times. Instead of retreating to her office when she had a break to do paperwork, she hung out in the front, watching Mona like a hawk.

By the time the last patient left for the day, Beth felt on edge and in no mood to present the gifts she'd brought in this morning. They weren't necessary, but face-to-face talks were.

"Vanessa, would you join me in my office," she said. "Noah and Mona, please stick around. I need to talk to each of you, too."

Vanessa followed her down the hall, and Beth

shut the door behind them to insure privacy. Vanessa looked scared to death.

Beth touched her arm reassuringly and said, "You're not in trouble, Vanessa. Sit down for a minute. I just want this chance to say thank you."

Vanessa collapsed in a chair. "I thought you were going to fire me."

"Fire you?" Regret swelled in Beth's chest. She'd done a very bad job if Vanessa thought that. "I can't imagine what we would do without you. I brought you a little gift this morning and planned to present it, along with Noah's and Mona's, in a little appreciation ceremony, but this has been an unusual day."

"Everyone has been so quiet!"

"There's a reason. At lunch, I learned that I haven't been doing my job."

"What do you mean? I love the changes you've made, Dr. Beth."

"Thank you, but what I'm saying is, I've let some things slide that created impossible stress for you and Noah. I'm not blind to that anymore."

"Ohh, you mean Mona."

Beth didn't feel right talking to one employee specifically about another, but this had to be said. "Vanessa, if you see anything that doesn't seem right, I want to know about it. You won't get in trouble. Don't be afraid to speak up."

"I can tell you anything?"

Beth nodded. What else was there?

"I do have one thing…if I'm not going to get in trouble…."

"You're not."

"Dr. Beth, I don't think you've noticed…"

Another failure?

"Noah can't keep his eyes off you."

What? Beth stared, stupefied. She hadn't expected that.

"I've never seen Noah the way he is with you. He smiles, he jokes. I don't think he knows it yet, but he's crazy about you."

"Well, yes, we're becoming good friends," Beth acknowledged, trying to hide how flustered—and delighted—she was.

Vanessa bit her lip to hold back a smile. "I know you have to say you're just friends, but I see what I see. You two are going to make a great couple."

Vanessa deserved a bigger gift than replacement candy! Beth gave her what she had and said, "Would you send Noah in, and would you stay with Mona until I send for her?"

"I sure will, and that's a good idea about me staying. Noah and I try not to leave Mona alone."

Beth wanted to beat her head against her desk. She had been *so* blind. Even Vanessa knew there was a problem while Beth lived in a bubble of Jesus' love and goodwill. There had to be a balance between loving people and seeing that they didn't hurt others.

Chapter Thirteen

"You wanted to see me?" Noah stood at the door, focusing somewhere over her head.

She motioned him in and closed the door. How could she talk to a man who wouldn't even look at her? Walking to the window, she stared outside, gathering her thoughts. "Noah, I don't know how to say this, but I am so sorry—"

He touched her arm. "You're sorry?"

She caught her breath at his touch and turned to see the remorse in his eyes.

"I'm the one who's sorry," he said. "Beth, you don't have anything to be sorry about."

"But I was so angry in Grandpa's office."

"And you had a right to be! You walked into a bad situation here that neither Keith nor your grandfather expected. When Mona stayed on, and it looked like things could get rough, what could they do? They're men of integrity, Beth. You know that. No one meant to belittle you or disrespect you. The intention was to get Mona out of here without involving you in a problem you didn't create."

His loyalty to Grandpa was worthy of respect. "I think I understand all that now, and I appreciate what you've done...though I still regret that you had to do it."

He rubbed the back of his neck as if tension had built up there. "When the chief brought me into the situation, I wasn't sure I could spy on someone. Then I saw how Mona treated you and how nice you were in return, and I not only wanted to help, I was honored to help."

"Really?" Wisps of happiness rose in Beth's heart, and she wished they were the couple that Vanessa had predicted. She could use a hug after the day they'd had.

"Beth, you've come in here and swept us off our feet with your kindness. This last weekend, I had more fun than I've had in ages. Kendi is crazy about you. All she can talk about is the Mother-Daughter Tea. Harlene thinks you're wonderful. Vanessa thinks you're the greatest, and I L-O-V-E, love working for you."

Kendra's phrase made her smile—as he intended, but the sincerity of his comforting words brought back that trouble with her knees. She reached out to him, just for support, but he took her in his arms and held her, his chin against her forehead…for a second, maybe two.

For him, it was probably just a reassuring, supportive, I'm-here-for-you hug. She shouldn't read more into it than that, but she looked up and found him gazing at her with strong emotion that was neither reassurance nor support.

That look took her breath and made her knee problem much worse. It was a good thing he was there to hold on to. His eyes drifted to her mouth, and she'd never wanted a kiss more in her life.

"Beth," he whispered.

She loved the way he said her name.

"Mona's waiting."

Talk about a splash of cold water! Beth stepped out of his arms and wondered how she was supposed to keep things professional when her senses were reeling?

She had to see Mona, but first she would give Noah his present. That would make a nice transition from irrational romance to office reality.

"What's this?" he said, peering through the plastic wrapper. "A kite?"

She pointed to the picture on the package. "It's a promise rainbow…for you and Kendra."

He looked at her as if she'd done something

wonderful, which made her feel that she had. When he reached for her, she tipped her head up for the kiss she longed for.

But he cupped her head in his big hand and pulled her close for a kiss on her forehead—not exactly the location she'd had in mind.

"I'll be close by while you're talking to Mona," he said, moving toward the door. "You're not alone."

"Thank you," she said, sitting in her big leather desk chair. When she talked to Mona, she needed every inch of authority and professionalism she could muster. The lollipops in her chest pocket should go in the drawer.

Mona sashayed into the office as though she owned the place, and she probably felt as if she did, as long as she'd worked here. "It looks like you're passing out presents," she said with a smirk.

That smirk sent oceans of courage zipping through Beth's veins.

"I hope it's not those flowers," Mona said, holding her nose. "You know how allergic I am."

"You won't be here long enough for your allergy to kick in. Please, have a seat."

Mona checked her watch. "I don't have time to chat. You seem to have forgotten I have seniority here. You shouldn't have made me wait."

Beth was in no mood to have Mona standing

over her in the power position. "Have a seat, Mona, unless you plan for this to be your last day."

Mona rolled her eyes and made a sound of amused disgust, but she sat.

"Mona, I know you *can* be a loyal professional. You were a credit to Keith. However, in the last two weeks, you have been neither loyal nor professional working with me."

"I *beg* your pardon!" Mona said with fire in her eyes.

"Actually, that's quite appropriate. You should beg my pardon. You've done things that warrant an apology. Fortunately for you, I'm willing to give you another chance. Singular. One chance. Take it or leave it. Be the kind of nurse I know you can be...or you won't be working here anymore. Do you understand?"

Outraged, Mona blinked once, which might have meant yes, but she sashayed out with the same arrogant confidence with which she'd come in.

Beth reached for Mona's very expensive, gourmet chocolate truffles, broke the seal on the box, chose one of the tempting treats and bit in. Creamy, rich chocolate melted in her mouth. Poor Mona. She didn't know what she was missing.

Noah came back, a worried frown on his face. "Didn't you talk to Mona?"

"I gave her an ultimatum and one more chance, as I said I would do."

"She walked out of here as if she'd won the round. Are you okay?"

Beth shrugged. "I'm not okay enough to let Mona have these." She held the box of candy out, inviting him to share Mona's present.

He perched on the edge of her desk and popped a truffle in his mouth. His eyes widened with pleasure. "Whoa! These are really good."

"Take two." She shoved the box his way.

"Mona doesn't know what she's missing."

"My thought exactly! But I don't think she cares. She has an agenda, Noah, and she's not going to come around. I really did want to show her God's love."

"I think you have."

"It hasn't seemed to make any difference."

"That's hard to measure. Other people have seen how you live. It may have made a difference to them."

Little Bethie showed her true colors today, but it had only been a matter of time. With all of her talk about God, she was as bad as the rest of the Brennans—even that fool, Trey, who she'd played like a fish, baiting him with her "concern" about his sister's competence.

Beth's ridiculous ultimatum might make it more difficult to do what had to be done, but the Brennans could not rip Keith out of her life the way they'd taken his picture from the staff photo gallery. He was in her heart to stay.

She needed to talk to her beloved so badly, she sometimes thought she would die. They hadn't been apart this long since their love was new. How lonely Keith must be without her.

Tonight he would surely be back from his fishing trip, and she would catch a glimpse of him. She lived for the moments when she saw him at the kitchen-sink window or relaxing in his living room on her daily drive-by. That he seldom closed the drapes or pulled the shades was a clear signal of how much he needed their love to live on.

She turned her car onto Keith's street and felt excitement rise in her chest. This was the best part of her day. Keith was waiting for her, longing for her, hoping to see her. Today, he might stop her and admit what they both knew. He couldn't live without her.

There it was—his home—with the low-slung roof line and the sleek architectural design. What was that in the yard? A For Sale sign? That was brand-new! It hadn't been there yesterday. And the house looked deserted.

Panic sent her heart racing. She could manage if Keith wasn't at home, but if he didn't live here at all, what would she do?

She would rise to the occasion. That's what! She was not a woman who crumbled at life's little adversities. Love made her strong...and resourceful.

She would call the phone number on the sign and make an appointment with the real estate agent. If that didn't provide the information she needed, she would dip into her savings and hire a private investigator. She would find Keith, no matter where the Brennans had hidden him away.

On Thursday evening, Beth and Kendra ordered chicken strips and French fries in the mall food court. While they waited, Beth asked, "Kendra, have you ever prayed before you go shopping?"

Kendra looked startled. "Are we supposed to?"

Beth smiled. Kendra did love to play by the rules, like a true only child. "Some people wait to pray until they have something really big to ask God about."

"Yep. Like bunions," Kendra said, nodding wisely. "Harlene says, 'God, heal my bunions.'"

"And that's good! But God says we're supposed to ask for help for everything, even finding the right dress."

When Kendra prayed for their food, she included her shopping need, too. Beth smiled to herself, wondering what Kendra would add to her prayer list the next time she prayed in Noah's presence.

They finished eating, and Kendra put her hand in Beth's as they walked down the mall corridor. Beth loved the feel of that little hand.

At the upscale department store where Beth's mother used to bring her when she was little, they walked by the cosmetic counter. A sales rep surprised Kendra with the offer of a squirt of designer perfume. Near the escalator, a musician in evening dress played classics on a grand piano.

"Where are the shopping carts?" Kendra looked around. "Aren't we supposed to have a cart? I can push it."

"Do you and Daddy shop in places where they have everything—like food, clothes, tools, shampoo—"

Kendra nodded. "And toys. I look at the toys."

"I'm afraid this store just has clothes, and no shopping carts."

Like a good girl, Kendra tried to hide her low opinion of such an inferior store. They boarded the escalator, and she said, "It would be hard to take a cart up these stairs."

Who wouldn't love this smart little girl? Beth led the way to the girls' department and looked for a rack of party dresses. Kendra let go of Beth's hand and moved quickly through the department.

In a flash, she was back, her face sorrowful. "No yellow," she reported as if it were a tragedy.

Beth held a pink dress in one hand and a lavender one in the other. "You would look beautiful in these."

Kendra looked doubtful.

"Why don't we try another store?" They had a couple of hours before Kendra would get sleepy.

The second upscale department store in the mall was just as disappointing in their failure to stock the color of choice, but a charming children's boutique had three yellow dresses in Kendra's size! She tried on her favorite and looked into the mirror with awe.

"You look beautiful, Kendra. Do you like this one?"

"I think I look like a princess," the child said shyly.

Beth knelt beside her and looked into the mirror, too. "Do you feel like a princess?"

Kendra nodded her head.

"Then this is your dress."

Kendra leaned against Beth and tears welled in her eyes. "I wish you were my mommy."

Beth took the little girl in her arms and stroked her hair, swamped by a fierce rush of love. Where were the words to answer this child's longing? Was there anything she could say other than promise to make this little girl's wish come true?

That wasn't a promise Beth could make. If there were words, they had to be spoken in a prayer for God's will, not theirs. God might have Kendra's mommy waiting in the wings, though Beth was right here, volunteering for the role.

Lord, you know I love Kendra. If you have another plan for her, for me, help us understand. Talk to Noah, Lord. Help him to see the possibilities.

When Noah thought about it, it was the Mother-Daughter Tea invitation two weeks ago that had turned his life upside-down. Or maybe it was that whole weekend. That's when Beth had gone to pizza night for the first time, and the next day, she'd won Harlene's heart. By the middle of the next week, when Beth and Kendi went shopping for the new yellow dress—and brought back a pink one, too—his and Kendi's old routine was done for. If Beth wasn't along, his sweet little daughter turned into a grouch.

It didn't help that Beth seemed to have very little social life beyond the one she had with them. She ate mac and cheese at their house; they swam in her pool; Friday-night pizza at Sluggers and Tuesday-night tacos at Adolph's were set dates.

Kendi was so in love with Beth that anyone could see it, and Beth returned her love. It almost hurt to watch them together, they were so much alike.

This evening they were going to the beach, their second trip in two weeks. Although the ocean was less than an hour away, he'd rarely gone since he met Merrilee. She hadn't been a sand-between-your-toes kind of woman and his single-dad weekends had been too full of chores for him to take Kendi.

But just last Saturday, he'd rented a pair of bikes at the pier—one for himself and the other, a tandem with the front seat for Beth and a child-sized rear seat for Kendi. He'd ridden behind them and enjoyed the view. The ocean was bluer than blue, and the girls—that was what Kendi liked to call herself and Beth—looked adorable in their bike helmets.

After hot dogs and ice cream, Kendi drew a big rainbow in the sand while Beth made a castle and he took a nap—or pretended to. There'd been a lot of giggles and whispers while they buried him in the sand.

He smiled, thinking of how Kendi had squealed when he jumped up, grabbed her hand and Beth's and ran for the surf to splash off some of that sand. He should have made the effort to make Kendi that happy long before now, but it didn't come naturally to him as it did with Beth.

His daughter sat in the back seat of Beth's yellow VW. She wore her sunglasses with the green rims because she couldn't find her yellow ones—a loss that created high drama. Beth sat in the passenger seat, her face turned to the late-afternoon sun, catching up on her sleep. Emergencies had kept her up most of the night.

And he had the privilege of driving the Beetle. It took a manly man to sit behind the wheel of this little car with the top down while traffic on the Santa Monica Freeway blew right past him. He would have preferred his SUV, but Beth and Kendi wanted the convertible, and they generally got their way, though he'd put his foot down about what he would wear.

Kendi wanted them to be the yellow family again, but not even for her would he meet Beth's friends and family as the daddy of the yellow family. It wasn't just how silly he felt, wearing matching clothes, he didn't want anyone to get the wrong idea about how he saw his and Beth's futures.

They were friends, really good friends, who'd only known each other one month. Four weeks. Not long at all if he didn't count those few minutes he and Beth had shared a year and a half ago.

If she'd begun her practice at BMC then, would their friendship have developed the way it had? Probably not. His grief had still been too new, and his daughter hadn't been mommy-shopping then. That was for sure.

Now Kendi's feelings for Beth rocketed way past friendship, though he could hardly blame her when he had a difficult time himself keeping the proper perspective. Beth only had to look at him for him to feel unhinged, and he couldn't stop thinking about the kiss that had almost happened.

There hadn't been a repeat of that moment, but she'd slipped her hand in his several times. Usually, she was holding hands with Kendi, too, which made it seem natural. She didn't have to know that when she took his hand, his heart always raced.

Even more often, she would touch his arm, his shoulder, his back, but he reminded himself that Beth was a toucher. She did the same thing with Vanessa and their patients, though he was pretty sure she didn't look at them the same way. He knew so little about love that he didn't know what was going on between them, but when their eyes met, he couldn't look away, not if his life depended upon it.

The power of his love for Kendi…that he definitely understood. The deep affection he'd felt for Merrilee…he got that, too. But what he felt for Beth blurred the lines of friendship and this other feeling until he didn't know what to think or what to do…other than follow her lead.

That was like walking on shifting sand. Merrilee had teased him about being a control freak. Admittedly, he didn't take it well when the unexpected came at him sideways. He preferred to be the leader, and anything else made him uneasy.

Glancing over at Beth, so near in this little car, his heart bumped hard against his chest. Like Kendi, he wanted to be with her all the time, and he wondered if he'd ever get the opportunity to hold her again.

Last night, Beth had talked about her dad a little, or about how little he'd been around as she grew up. Like everyone at Cedar Hills, Noah had known that Dr. James T. Brennan, Jr. seemed to live there. Beth confirmed what the rumor mill said about her mother's problems. They were a mix of psychological disorders that had made her family's life a nightmare.

That gave Noah the guts to share that his dad had been some teenage guy who his teenage mom couldn't remember, and that she'd left him with Grandpa McKnight when Noah had been a baby. His grandfather had given him a good home for eight years, until he'd passed away. His drugged-out mother had showed up just often enough that he hadn't been adoptable, but mostly, she'd lived her life in and out of prison on drug-related charges while he'd lived his life wherever the state placed him.

If there had been an ounce of pity in Beth's eyes, he couldn't have shared all that, but he was glad he had. Keeping his past a secret hadn't felt right, not when they'd been spending so much time together.

If it bothered her, she sure didn't show it. In fact, she'd looked at him with admiration and said, "Your grandfather would be so proud at the way you've turned out."

That put a lump in his throat.

Tonight would be a test of sorts. The people attending Ry's beach birthday party were totally out of his league. Beth promised he would have a great time, but he was a bundle of nerves. Her brother Ry had broken the mold and become a paramedic, which gave them something in common, but Meg was an assistant TV producer of a nationally televised show, her brother Pete was a millionaire land developer and his wife, Sunny, was the daughter of a former United States senator!

If that wasn't enough to intimidate a guy, the party was at a beach house in Malibu! Movie stars and the very rich lived out there, not guys like Noah. He'd ridden through on a sightseeing trip once with Merrilee, and he'd felt like a trespasser just doing that.

How was he supposed to fit in at a party like this? Grandpa had taught him that he was as good as anyone. Most of the time, Noah believed it. He didn't care if people were important or wealthy, but these people mattered to Beth. He didn't want to let her down.

He nudged her awake to point out Sunny and Pete's beach house, and she looked at him with a sleepy, loving smile that made his heart turn over.

The house was one of the more modest beachfront homes, though modest was a relative term. He could never afford to live in such a place. He turned into the driveway and said, "Kendi, we're here," but he wished they weren't.

He felt just like he used to when he'd arrive at the door of a new set of foster parents, wondering if this time it would work out. It never did, though his social worker would say it wasn't his fault. Maybe not, but when it happened more than once, a guy had to wonder.

But the door opened, and Noah was met with hugs from Meg and Sunny, warm handshakes from Ry and, a kiss from two-year-old Meggy who rode high on Pete's arm and a manly high five from five-year-old Shay. He was greeted like an old friend, not somebody new.

Vaguely, he noticed that Kendi and Beth were receiving the same fantastic, warm greeting. No wonder Beth said these people were her real family. The love in this house was a tangible thing.

Beth and Kendi passed out the gift bags they'd brought—birthday presents to Ry and toys for Pete and Sunny's children. Sunny took Kendi with her children to a play area in the kitchen, and Pete led the rest of them through a light-filled living area to an awesome deck overlooking the ocean.

It was like something he might have seen in a movie. Flowers bloomed in colorful pots. There was a hammock big enough for two, cushioned lounge chairs, a big table covered with an umbrella, a huge grill—all of it fantastic, but even more impressive was the beach beneath the deck, the rhythmic sound of the surf and the view of endless sea.

"Make yourself at home, Noah," Pete said, taking a platter of thick raw hamburger patties from Meg. "We were just waiting for you before we put on the burgers."

"I've already made myself at home," Ry said, stretching out on the hammock. "Wake me up for dinner."

Noah smiled. Catching a nap whenever possible was a trait common to medics.

"Can I help?" he asked, impressed with the size of the grill. Besides the beef patties, there was corn on the cob, a foil-covered pan that Pete said was garlic potatoes, zucchini slices and a pan of melted butter.

Pete handed him a pair of tongs. "My dad always said, 'Treat your guests like family.' Sure, you can help."

Noah looked around to check on Kendi and Beth. Beth stood near the kitchen, watching him with a big smile on her face. Kendi was playing with Shay and baby Meggy nearby. Beth gave him a little wave as if to say she could see he was doing fine, and she turned to go in the kitchen.

Amazingly, his uneasiness was gone. With a pair of tongs in his hand, he felt right at home.

Chapter Fourteen

Noah had never experienced anything like this birthday dinner for Ry. These people could have chosen to celebrate any way they wanted, but they sat around the table on the deck, all nine of them—the grown-ups and the kids—eating burgers and corn on the cob. It could have been any family gathering, except for the waves lapping the shore and the setting sun turning the sky to lavender, coral and gold.

Conversation flowed easily, broken often with laughter, which the birthday guy had a lot to do with. Ry had a great sense of humor and told the best stories. He also made sure no one was left out, not baby Meggy, not young Shay and definitely not Kendra. Ry had her telling things about her daddy that were slightly embarrassing, but Noah only pretended to mind.

These people came from money, but money couldn't buy the love at this table. The two sets of siblings—Pete and Meg, Ry and Beth—had also been neighbors as they grew up. They shared a lifetime of memories, and they shared the same faith, the same values, even the same church.

They'd brought Sunny into their fold, and they made him and Kendi feel welcome, too. Was there anything he wanted more for Kendi than a family like this?

Before they'd eaten, they'd joined hands, and Kendi had been asked to say grace—probably because Beth suggested it. Naturally, Kendi mentioned each of them in her prayer and itemized the food to be blessed, stretching out the prayer. She'd ended with, "God bless the birthday boy!"

There had been applause after that, and Beth had looked proud. Asking for the blessing might be more of a ritual than a real conversation with the Lord, but he appreciated the way they made Kendi feel special.

For dessert, Meg brought a tall cake to the table and set it in front of Ry. Except for red letters that spelled out, Happy Birthday Ry, the cake was all white.

"Ah, wedding cake, my favorite," Ry said, rising from his chair to steal a kiss from his wife.

"It's only been his favorite since we were married," Meg said, laughing at the way he nuzzled her neck. "White cake and white icing—that's what Ry likes."

"And I'll enjoy it again at Collin's wedding."

"I could understand why Collin asked his cousin Ry to be his best man," Beth said, "but I'm still surprised the bride asked me to be an attendant, too. We didn't meet until her bridal shower, but she said she wanted to include Collin's family."

"I'm covering the guest book," Meg added.

"We're going," Sunny said, "though neither of us know Collin's bride. What's her name? Linda?"

"Glenda," Kendi corrected politely. "Me and Daddy know Glenda. We're going, and I'm wearing a pink dress!" She and Beth exchanged loving smiles.

"Kendra, can you talk Glenda into letting us all sit together at the reception?" Pete asked.

"Can I, Daddy?" his daughter asked, taking the request seriously.

He shrugged with a smile. Asking Glenda for a favor, as busy as she would be, this close to the wedding, wasn't his style, but it meant a lot that Pete had thought of the idea.

Before Ry cut his cake, they all joined hands again and took turns, praying for Ry. They began with baby Meggy and Shay who were coached to say, "God bless Uncle Ry."

As they went around the table, Noah felt the pressure. His turn was coming. What should he do?

This was not the time or place to admit he had doubts that God listened to prayers, nor had he ever voiced those doubts. He'd gone to church and read the Bible enough to remember a person wasn't supposed to cause another to stumble in their faith.

Should he fake faith for this occasion and come up with words that would sound okay? That would be polite, though it seemed wrong.

Maybe he could borrow their faith for a moment and speak sincerely to the Lord they believed in.

When it was his turn, he said, "Lord, thank You for the way Ry shows his love for You. Even without him saying how much he loves You, it's easy to see."

Beth looked Noah's way, her eyes full of admiration, appreciation, approval—any and all of which would make him feel wonderful if guilt didn't churn in his stomach.

Ry sliced and plated the cake. Meg passed it around, and Sunny passed a crystal bowl of round scoops of ice cream in a variety of flavors and colors.

Kendi crawled up in Noah's lap and whispered in his ear, "Daddy, that was a good prayer."

Kendi meant that as a good thing, but he felt such guilt, that his child would praise him for a simple prayer. Kendi hadn't heard him pray in a long time, maybe not since her mother had died. She snuggled in his arms until ice cream and cake lured her away.

Beth could hardly wait to get Meg's and Sunny's impression of Noah. The opportunity came when the guys went in the house to put the children to bed.

Sunny gave her a hug and said, "Beth, I've never seen you so happy, and now I know the reason why. Noah is perfect, and his daughter is adorable."

Beth's smile was so wide, it almost hurt. "What did you think, Meg?" Meg's opinion had always been the one that mattered most.

"I think I called it. I knew you'd met someone."

Sunny and Beth groaned, but they didn't dispute Meg's claim. She did seem to have a knack for recognizing couple potential—which she used on her job, selecting the contestants for a TV dating game show.

"Noah's wonderful," Meg said sincerely, though without her usual bubbly enthusiasm. "If he were on *Dream Date,* he would be the star of the episode."

"But....?" Beth heard the qualifier coming.

"But how is his relationship with the Lord?"

"I'm sure it's okay," Beth answered, though she felt a check in her spirit. Did she really know that? "Noah doesn't talk about the Lord the way we do, but not all Christians do. You heard him and Kendra pray. They believe, and you see what a good person he is."

"Good person?" Meg repeated.

Beth sighed. "I know. Being good doesn't mean he knows the Lord, but it's a good indicator."

"Where does he go to church?" Sunny asked.

Meg was going to jump all over this answer. "He doesn't," Beth confessed. "He transports Kendra and their neighbor, Harlene, but he doesn't stay."

Sunny and Meg exchanged a glance, not surprisingly.

"Does he say why?" Meg asked.

"Those few hours are the only ones he has alone all week. You know how it is for single parents."

The answering silence said what Beth already knew. It wasn't a good enough reason. Single parents needed the fellowship of a good church as much as they needed time alone, if not more. "Maybe I should talk to Noah about this," she said. Nagging wasn't her style, but sometimes words should be said.

"Hon, you're asking for heartache if you commit to a man who isn't committed to the Lord," Meg said with love.

Beth believed that, too, but had she waited too long? Could she pull away from Noah now, especially when she'd promised to be Kendra's friend, whatever happened?

"When the guys come back, take Noah for a moonlit stroll on the beach," Sunny said. "Talk about the ocean, the stars, the tides, the God of the universe—and ask Noah if he knows the Lord personally."

"Once a teacher, always a teacher," Meg said dryly, kidding Sunny who'd taught and coached at the high-school level before she had kids.

"I'm sorry," Sunny said, chagrined. "It did sound like a lesson plan, didn't it?"

"That's okay," Beth said. "I need the help. Moonlight and Jesus. Do you really think they go together?"

Sunny reached out for their hands. "Let's ask the Lord about it and—"

"Surrender to the possibilities?" Beth said with a smile.

They laughed, knowing where she'd heard the phrase, and Meg repeated the words when she prayed. Shared faith and friendship were wonderful, powerful blessings.

Noah laid his sleeping daughter on the bed in the guest room, once again amazed at her talent for zonking out at the same time every night. He walked past the kids' rooms and saw that Uncle Ry had planned to rock baby Meggy to sleep, but he was the one snoozing while the tiny redhead listened to her daddy read a book to her brother.

Noah walked quietly down the stairs, admiring the skylights and the open spaciousness of the living area. It was awesome to think that Pete had worked for his dad when the two of them had built this house. Back then, Pete said, he'd never dreamed of owning a home like this.

In one corner of the deck, Beth, Meg and Sunny were holding hands, praying. Man, these people prayed a lot. He walked to the edge of the deck, leaned on the rail and stared at the ocean. Deck lights from the adjoining houses provided some illumination, but, mostly, he stared into dark nothingness, enjoying the sound of the sea.

Beth joined him and slipped her arm around his waist, almost as if she were claiming him. Would she do that in front of her family? He couldn't help glancing around to see if they were alone. They almost were. Meg and Sunny worked in the kitchen that opened onto the deck.

He slid his arm around Beth and looked down at her pretty face. Wisps of hair blew across her eyes. He smoothed them back, which wasn't much of an excuse to touch her, but the only one he had.

At the touch of his hand, she gasped as if she were catching her breath. He knew that feeling. She looked up at him with such a loving expression that he wanted to sweep her up in his arms.

"Hey, you two," Sunny called from the kitchen. "Why don't you go for a stroll? I'll listen for Kendra."

Noah looked to Beth to get her reaction, but she was already shucking out of her yellow leather sneaks and heading for the stairs to the beach. He laughed, kicked off his shoes and followed her across the deep soft sand that oozed over his feet. She waited near the water's edge on the sand packed hard by the tides.

"That was nice of Sunny," he said. "Which way shall we go? Left or right?"

"How about right? Everything seems right tonight."

When he was with Beth, it always seemed right, but he couldn't say that out loud. Besides it sounded too simple for the way he felt about her. For the first time, he took her hand before she took his. It was way past his turn. He tried to remember they were supposed to be friends and no more, but that was like ignoring the stars sparkling on this perfect night.

"Everyone loved you and Kendra," Beth said, sounding as if she were short of breath though they walked at strolling pace.

"Your brother and your friends are great," he said, having the same trouble with respirations. "I love how you're all one happy family."

"They're your family, too, Noah. We don't share the same DNA, but we're all brothers and sisters in the Lord."

He knew what she was talking about. God was the Father. His son was Jesus Christ, and believers were Jesus' brothers and sisters—all of them, children of the Father. It was a concept Noah used to accept without question, and, in a way, he still did. He would rather believe it than believe nothing. "Pete and Sunny have a terrific place," he said, hoping to change the subject.

"When Pete bought this house, he was at the lowest point in his life. He'd lost everything that mattered, including his ability to do the job he loved. He'd had so many surgeries, his face wasn't even the same, and his faith was shattered. He bought the beach house with insurance settlement money, and hid away here, just counting seagulls, day after day."

That was startling to hear. Pete was a very good-looking guy—a person who made things happen. It was hard to believe he hadn't always known where he was going and how to get there.

"When Pete met Sunny, and she pointed him to a real relationship with Christ, he got a brand-new life."

Was Beth drawing a parallel between his life and Pete's? Granted, there were similarities. When he lost Merrilee, it was such a blow that doubt exploded and wouldn't leave him alone, but his faith wasn't totally shattered.

They walked in silence. He waited to see if Beth thought he was bright enough to catch on or if she needed to draw him a picture. Preaching would sure ruin a beautiful night.

When they came to the point where this stretch of the beach ended and it was time to turn back, she said, "Noah, do you think we could ever be more than friends?"

If he answered that honestly, wouldn't it change things between them so much that they could never get back to simple friendship? But how could he be less than honest? He turned to face her and said what he had to. "I think about it all the time."

"You do?" she said with a lilt in her voice.

He touched her face, and she leaned her cheek into his hand, closed her eyes and rubbed the corner of her mouth against his palm. It was such a little thing, but it gave him the courage to take her face in both of his hands. "Sometimes I wonder…"

"You wonder…?" Her eyes were on his mouth.

"I wonder what it would feel like…" He lowered his face toward hers slowly, giving her plenty of time to push him away.

But she didn't. She held his shoulders and raised her lips to meet his.

The touch of her mouth on his was as sweet as he'd dreamed of. It was just one soft touch, then another. Her arms stole around his neck, and she touched her cheek against his jaw before sliding her lips back to his mouth.

He'd known what it was like to be married and loved, but had he ever felt quite like this? If he had, how could he have forgotten it? There would be no forgetting these kisses.

Gently, slowly, she pulled back and buried her face against his pounding heart. She would hear his heart, even feel it, but it didn't matter. He wanted her to know what she meant to him. It was too soon for him to say he'd fallen for her, even to himself, but what else could this be?

* * *

Waiting for an usher to seat them at Collin and Glenda's elegant wedding, Noah felt like a fish out of water, but his poised little daughter seemed right at home. Of course she was thrilled with her poofy pink dress and her shiny pink shoes, but he was uncomfortable in his starched white dress shirt and dark suit. The last time he'd dressed up like this was for Merrilee's funeral.

A teenage usher, the nephew of the bride, offered Kendi his arm, and she took it just the way she'd seen other ladies do. Noah followed them down the aisle, smiling that Kendi was getting the chance to play the part of princess for an audience of more than himself. They were seated on the bride's side, and Noah nodded to several people he knew from Cedar Hills Hospital.

Ry and Meg had mentioned that they'd been married in this lush garden chapel next to their church, but they'd had only a dozen or so guests. Today the garden was filled with at least two hundred white folding chairs, and it looked as if the guests were the Who's Who of Brennan Medical Clinic and Cedar Hills Hospital.

A string ensemble played very pretty music, not classical—he recognized a tune or two from church—but it sounded classy. Overhead, birds sang an accompaniment to the music and the low hum of pre-wedding chatter.

"Hi, Noah." Darcy Jacobsen, a nurse who'd worked the ER with him and Glenda, slid across him and Kendi. "This young lady can't be your daughter, Noah. Hi there, pretty girl."

Kendi gave him a quizzical look.

"Darcy's a nurse friend of Glenda's and mine," he said.

"I'm a nurse, too," Kendi told Darcy.

"Kendi called in the 911 for our neighbor, Harlene," he explained.

"Oh, sweetie, good for you. You're going to make a good nurse someday, just like Daddy."

"Or a ped-i-a-tri-cian," Kendi enunciated carefully, "like Beth."

"Your boss?" Darcy murmured with lifted eyebrows.

He nodded. "A great role model."

"Any truth to the rumor that she's been auditioning for a more maternal role?" she said with a glance at Kendi.

"Beth and Kendi are very good friends," he said, putting a limitation on that rumor.

"That sounds like the public statement. Now, what's the real story?"

"We *are* good friends," Kendi said with a frown.

There. That was telling it like it was.

"I'm sure you are, sweetie."

"You can call me Kendra."

Darcy grimaced playfully, acknowledging she'd just been shot down.

If there was a "real story," Darcy should know he wouldn't tell it. He hated gossip and the damage it did. "Have you ever seen so many pink flowers?" he asked his daughter.

"It's a very pink wedding," she answered seriously.

He nodded as the first of the wedding party came down the aisle.

Kendi leaned across him, the better to see the bridesmaids approaching. "There's Beth!" she whispered, waving at Beth discreetly.

Beth spotted them, smiled and winked at Kendi...or him. It was hard to tell. He smiled back anyway. How could he not? Beth looked so beautiful, she just blew him away.

The way the wedding party was lined up on either side of the landscaped archway, Beth faced the bride. That gave him the luxury of looking at Beth as much as he wanted without worrying that she would notice.

He took full advantage of the opportunity and caught every little move—the time she wiped a tear from her eye, the time she pressed her lips tight as if she was trying hard not to laugh, the look of sympathy when Collin nervously stumbled over Glenda's name.

When Collin and Glenda walked back down the aisle, the wedding party followed. Beth winked at Kendi again, but for an instant, her eyes locked with his.

Darcy tugged on his sleeve. She wore a knowing smile as she whispered over the top of Kendi's head, "Glenda hit the jackpot, marrying a Brennan, and it looks like you could, too! Way to go, Noah!"

He'd never liked Darcy much, and she'd sure ruined a nice moment…though that *was* what others would say when they saw Beth and him together at the reception. The gossips could go on for days with no more fuel than the sight of an unlikely couple who were just friends—a doctor and her nurse—sharing wedding cake.

Beth scooted out of the white limousine, ready to get soaked by the driving rain that had started after the wedding, but the wedding coordinator had planned ahead. Young men stood by with huge white umbrellas to keep the wedding party and guests dry as they entered the lobby of the Cathedral Hills Country Club.

Whether it was the unexpected rain in this dry

season, the contagious joy of the bridal couple or the fact that, in a matter of minutes, she would be sitting with the most handsome man at this wedding, Beth knew she'd never felt happier.

Before they left the church, she'd had a moment with Sunny who reported that Noah's eyes had been on Beth during the entire ceremony. And they both knew what that meant.

Collin and Glenda had chosen not to have a receiving line or a head table for the wedding party. They and their parents planned to greet their guests at the tables during the meal, and the wedding party was allowed to sit with their spouses, family and friends. It was going to be so much more fun, being part of the party instead of sitting on a dais, watching it.

Today marked the very last time Beth would be a bridesmaid, at least, the last time before she was a bride herself. She'd met the man she wanted to love and to cherish, and she was ready to say the rest of the wedding words!

Noah might not be quite that far along in his thinking, but the intense awareness they shared every day at work and most evenings with Kendra could end only one way—and there would be no long engagement or elaborate wedding.

The schedule said they had twenty minutes to freshen up before the grand entrance of the wedding party, and the ladies' room was a beehive of activity. The same makeup artists and hair stylists who'd worked their wonders before the wedding now fluffed, smoothed, sprayed and buffed with the precision of a surgical team. Beth had to respect that. A look in the mirror said they'd worked wonders. If she couldn't wow her guy looking this good, what would it take?

As each couple was introduced to polite applause, Beth scanned the room, looking for Noah. There he was! And his eyes were steady on her with a look that said he loved what he saw. That took the strength right out of her knees, and she clasped the arm of her groomsman partner for support.

She looked for Kendra, knowing her little love would be somewhere, waiting to catch her eye. There…at the kids' table, Kendra waved excitedly. Beth waved back, as proud of this child as a real mom would be.

The bride and groom were introduced, and the wedding party broke formation. Ry put a brotherly hand at the small of her back and steered her toward their table. "Oh, no!" he muttered in disgust.

"What?" It took a lot for Ry to lose his cool.

"It looks like Pete got his wish. All of us from my birthday party are sitting together, but it must be the cousins' table. See who else is there?"

Beth's heart sank. She loved Isabel, but Trey was

hard to take. There was an empty chair between
him and Noah, and there was another one between
Isabel and Meg. If it were anyone but Noah, she
would have hopped into the seat between the
women and let Ry fend for himself. Had Trey ever
gone for as long as ten minutes without zapping her
with criticism? She'd better pray now.

*Lord, let this be a joyful time for Collin and
Glenda. Help me keep my attitude right, and work
Your wonders with Trey. May our actions bring
him closer to You.*

Chapter Fifteen

At their table, she said, "Before I sit down, I'm just going to check on Kendra."

"I'll go with you," Noah said quickly, as if he might be grateful for the chance to escape. But they'd walked only steps away when he said, "Beth, Trey's been drinking."

"Drinking?" Beth was shocked.

"No doubt about it. You'll see for yourself."

There wouldn't be a drop of alcohol at this party, nor was it ever served at Brennan parties. Her grandfather had set the example years ago, and her family followed it still.

At the kids' table, Kendra was in her element, playing unofficial hostess, but she reached up her arms for a hug from Beth.

"Are you having fun?" Beth asked, smoothing

tendrils of hair off the child's forehead and wishing the problem of Trey would go away.

"*Lots* of fun! We have a clown instead of a babysitter!"

Beth laughed, recognizing the clown in her funny makeup and pink-and-white wedding costume. She ought to. Chloe Kilgannon volunteered often in the children's wing of Cedar Hills Hospital. Her dad was chief of staff there.

It was just like the quiet, intelligent woman to play with the kids at the wedding rather than sit with her gorgeous, gregarious sisters and outgoing parents. Chloe held up a sign that said, "Hi," and flipped it around to say, "Bye."

Beth blew her a kiss and told Noah, "Kendra's in good hands."

He waved at Kendra and tucked Beth's hand in the crook of his elbow, turning them back toward their table.

"I like the suit," she said admiringly, "but I really should have gotten you a pink tie to match Kendra and me."

"Not even for you would I have worn a pink tie," he said, squeezing her hand, "but you could talk me into just about anything else. You look beautiful, Beth."

"Is it the hairdo or the makeup?" she teased, enjoying the freedom to flirt.

"Neither. It's how happy you look," he said seriously. "I love to see that."

A sweeping feeling that had to be love claimed every bone in her body and stamped a forever feeling in her heart. A kiss would be perfect right now.

"Hey, you two, save it for later," Ry teased with an approving smile. "I may only be an intern, but I can recognize a case of wedding fever when I see it."

"Who's got a fever? There's a doc-tor in the house. Lots of doc-tors. Seven Bren-nan doc-tors." Trey's words were slurred as he rose unsteadily to his feet. "Sit down, Doc-tor Brennan," he said to Beth. "You don't have a frog on your head, so you can sit by me."

Isabel tugged on his sleeve. "C'mon, Trey. Sit down. You're embarrassing yourself."

He sat, and so did Beth and Noah, but it was as if the others felt as paralyzed as Beth did. Trey seemed like a ticking bomb, ready to explode if any of them said the wrong thing. She'd never seen him like this.

Isabel had. Beth could see the fear on her face.

"Did I mention that this table is for Bren-nans…just Brennans?" he asked, looking pointedly at Sunny, Pete and Noah—especially Noah.

"Please, Trey," Beth said quietly, her hand on

his arm. "Be nice." If they got through this reception, she would never voluntarily spend time in Trey's company again.

"You're not fam'ly," he said, pointing to the non-Brennan three, "not unlesh you wear a frog on your head."

"Trey, you must think you're being funny," she said, embarrassed and angry as well, "but you're not."

"Should I take him outside?" Noah asked in her ear.

Pete was half out of his chair, when Ry rose and muttered, "I'll take care of this."

Beth could see Collin heading their way.

Ry circled the table, his face grim. "Let's take a walk, Trey."

"You take a walk," Trey said loudly, rising unsteadily again. "C'mon, Izzie, we're not sitting with people who aren't Brennans."

Rage blasted through Beth's best intentions. Trey was a drunken idiot. She was in no mood to pray, but she could manage one word. *"Jesus."* There was power in His name.

"Hey, Trey." Collin took Trey firmly by the arm. "Are you trying to ruin my wedding?"

"Not me!" Trey tried to shake Collin's arm off.

Ry took Trey's other arm. "See, Trey, it's just us three Brennan boys, going for a walk." He and

Collin muscled Trey to the door. Beth's dad wasn't far behind.

Isabel sat in a puddle of misery. "Should I go with them?" she asked, wiping tears from her cheeks.

"Only if you want to," Beth said, sliding over to Trey's seat, the better to hug her sister-in-law. "How long has Trey been drinking, Isabel?"

"Since your mother was hospitalized," she answered, her eyes dark with anguish. "I think he knows he's a lot like her, but he never listens to anyone."

"Maybe he will now," Sunny said, taking Ry's chair on the other side of Isabel.

"You're not alone," Meg added, hovering behind Isabel.

The bride joined them. "What's going on?" she asked sympathetically.

Fresh tears spilled onto Isabel's cheeks. "I'm sorry if we've ruined your wedding, Glenda, but I don't think I can stay."

Glenda took Isabel in her arms. "It's okay. When Trey learns to love the Lord, things will be different."

"Pete and I will take you home," Sunny said to Isabel.

Isabel lifted her chin. "I've been managing by myself ever since I married Trey. I can do this alone."

Sunny, Meg and Beth stayed with Isabel until the parking valet brought her car round. Collin, Ry, Noah and Pete met them in the lobby and reported that Trey's dad was taking his son to get help.

"Poor dad," Ry said. "He's never been around when he should have, but he comes through in the worst of moments."

That was more generous than Beth felt. Neither her mother nor her brother had gotten the attention of her dad until they went too far.

"Do I look okay?" Collin asked, tugging on his white tie. "Not rumpled or anything?"

Beth kissed her cousin's cheek and straightened his tie. "You look terrific, and you have a beautiful bride. I'm proud of all of you." Her eyes swept all of the men, especially Noah.

As if no unpleasantness had ever happened, the reception went on, though Noah was very quiet—even for him. Everyone else at the table seemed to make an extra effort to make this a happy occasion.

When it was time for the best man to give his speech, Ry took the mike. "My cousin Collin is the quiet one of the family—so quiet, he puts people to sleep."

The audience tittered at the anesthesiology reference.

"But he's also the smart one. He talked Glenda

into marrying into the Brennan family, though she knows what we're like."

That drew a laugh...from everyone but Noah. Was he still upset at the trouble with Trey?

"As the best man, the best thing I can say comes from the Book of Jeremiah in the Bible. Glenda...Collin...the Word says God has a plan for your life—a plan for your good and not for disaster. That's a promise to build a life on."

Beth found Noah's hand. Did he realize that promise was for them, too?

"Hey!" Kendra slid between them and pointed to the window excitedly. "The rain's stopped, and there's a promise rainbow for the wedding!"

Beth translated for the rest of the table. "That means everything's going to turn out all right."

Noah walked Kendra back to her table—or that's where Beth thought he was going. When she looked, Kendra was there, but Noah had disappeared.

Noah hadn't planned on inviting Beth back to the house. He was in no mood to rehash the wedding or think about the future, but when he dropped her off at the church to get her car, Kendi begged to ride with her.

He didn't mind too much because Kendi would fall asleep in the car. He was about to say good-night to Beth when Kendi stirred and asked Beth to put her to bed. Beth, of course, was delighted.

He went into his room and shut the door. He couldn't wait to get out of this suit and into shorts and a T-shirt so he could feel like himself. A man could play the role of somebody he wasn't only so long. During the speech-making, he'd taken a walk and tried to convince himself that he was in the right place at the right time, but it hadn't helped. Trey didn't have to worry about him being a Brennan wannabe. Noah had counted the minutes until they could leave.

The lavishness of that wedding had been so far beyond his world that it had been a jolt to walk through the door of his own house and see the difference. Yet, that's what Beth saw every time she came here.

He knew she loved him. She wasn't a person who could hide her feelings. He loved her, too, but how long would she be happy, playing house with him and Kendi?

Did she think of them living here, with the discount-store furnishings he and Merrilee had been very grateful to afford? Or did she think he would turn his back on the life he'd worked hard for and be grateful that he'd "hit the jackpot?" He wished Darcy had never said that.

It would be like the new dresses Beth had

bought for Kendi. He'd insisted on paying for them, but Beth wouldn't tell him how much they cost. Using an outside figure of what he'd paid for Kendi's other dresses, he'd put the money in Beth's purse. Had he been wrong! The price tags told the true story. Each of those dresses cost more than he made in a day and five times the price of any other dress Kendi owned. He couldn't afford that, and he didn't want Kendi getting used to such luxury.

With Beth, his life and Kendi's was so much better than when they'd been on their own. It nearly killed him to think of what it was going to be like without Beth, but this evening had raised too many questions. This had to end.

He knew Kendi was hoping for—praying for—another wedding. He loved the thought of having Beth in his arms forever, but he hated the idea of "marrying a Brennan." He didn't want to take on that clan.

Her grandfather, Ry and Collin were great, but he couldn't see himself at family gatherings that included Trey and the rest of them. Poor Isabel and little J.T. would be better off with a Brennan-less life, and so would he and Kendi.

He sat on his sofa—his feet on the coffee table, his hands behind his head—and waited for Beth. For the last few nights, they'd cuddled on this sofa, but they wouldn't be cuddling tonight…or any other night.

Beth joined him, kicked her shoes off and showed him a rainbow picture Kendi had just given her.

He'd seen dozens—hundreds—of rainbows. He was pretty much rainbowed out.

"I'm like Kendra," Beth said, her mouth tilted in that smile he usually loved. "I need the comfort of knowing God is in control and that He keeps His promises. Like Ry said in his speech, the Lord has a plan for each of us—a plan for our good and not for evil."

It hadn't sounded like preaching when Ry had said it, but it did now. "Do you really believe that, Beth?"

"Of course I do."

"Then, what do you think God's plan was for Kendi's mother? Was His plan to snuff out her life in twenty-six years? Was Kendi supposed to grieve for her mommy until you came along?"

Noah's words were so unexpected and his attitude so harsh that Beth could barely breathe. He'd been through so much, he had a right to be angry, but why did his words sound like an attack, and why tonight?

She'd asked the Lord to bring Noah to a wonderful connection to Him. Was this God's way of answering that prayer? Was this her chance to help Noah find a personal relationship with Jesus? She wished Ry were here. He was very good at leading people to the Lord.

"God doesn't promise unlimited days," she said, praying for the right words. "He doesn't promise life as we think it should be, and sometimes we never understand what His purpose was."

"*If* He had a purpose," Noah murmured.

"Sometimes, when we look back, we *do* see His purpose. I didn't understand why Grandpa delayed my practice at the clinic, and I allowed myself to be very upset about it. When I came back, I realized I was much better prepared to do my job. Situations like that are great faith-builders."

"Or coincidence."

"Coincidence or God's plan—it's a choice which one you want to believe. What do you lose by choosing faith?" She smiled to soften the challenge.

But he wouldn't look at her. So much for charming him to the Lord. If this was her opportunity to talk to Noah about the Lord, she'd better go for it and tell it like it was.

"Noah, God asks you to trust that He knows what He's doing. He wants you to show your love for Him by clinging to Him in good times and bad. You're a father. When bad times come to your child—maybe even from choices Kendra's made—should she blame you? When you make a decision that hurts her, should she say you aren't her dad anymore?"

Noah threw her an impatient look, but she knew he'd understood the analogy between himself as a father and God.

"What if it's something you do for Kendra's good, but she doesn't see it that way?" Beth continued determinedly. "Is it okay for her to avoid you or be angry because she doesn't like your decision? When things are bad for Kendra, so bad you know she's hurting, do you want her to stay close where you can comfort her...or run away? How would you feel if she says the bad times mean you never loved her...that she's through with you...that you don't exist?"

"I don't know, Beth," he said quietly. "I'm not a smart doctor with all the answers, but I've got a question for you. How am I supposed to work for you after all that preaching?"

It couldn't have been as bad as he made it sound. "I'm sorry if I came on too strong," she said softly, loving him so.

"You have a right to believe what you want, but you act like you think you're 'part of God's plan' for me and Kendi, and I've got to tell you, Beth...I don't think so."

That was like a dagger in her heart. Her breath came in shuddering gasps. He didn't mean that. He couldn't.

"I know Kendi's crazy about you, and she's not going to like it when you and I don't spend time together, but—"

"What are you saying?" That sounded so final.

"I'm saying...I don't want us to hang out anymore."

"Just like that? One bad night wipes out all the good times we've had together?"

"I think it has to."

They'd been together almost every day, even on the weekends, and the evenings as well. All *three* of them had been together. Was he thinking about Kendra at all?

"Am I still allowed to take Kendra to the Mother-Daughter Tea next Thursday?"

"If you want to."

"I do," she said, struggling to keep her voice steady when her lips quivered. "I promised I would be her friend, no matter what happened between us. Noah, what did happen?"

For a minute she thought he wasn't going to answer, but he said, "At the wedding, one of my friends said it looked like I was going to "hit the jackpot" and marry a Brennan. Call me shallow or too proud, but I'm not the kind of man who'll look the other way while you pay the bills. I don't even want the luxuries you're used to."

"Luxuries! I drive a VW and wear sneakers to work. I chose one of the lowest-paying specialties in medicine. Luxury is hardly my thing."

"Then why would you buy my daughter not one, but two dresses? Beth, I saw how much those dresses cost. They're more than I would pay for Kendi's entire wardrobe. And why would you let me think I'd given you enough money to pay for them? You take money for granted."

"You're right. I didn't think about the price of the dresses. I just loved buying them for Kendra. I'm sorry. I made a mistake, but every couple has things to work out. As far as money goes…what does it matter who puts the most money into a joint account? Noah, I just want to love you and have you love me back."

He shook his head as if he didn't even hear her. "I'm a giver, not a taker, and I can't do this. I'm not the guy for you, Beth."

"Oh, Noah…."

He stood abruptly, cutting her off. "Consider this my resignation…from everything, including my job. I'll work out my notice. Even you ought to find a reason to fire Mona within a couple of weeks."

She really couldn't breathe. Somehow she managed to stumble to her car and drive out of sight before she pulled the car over and let the tears fall. She had definitely been wrong. Noah was not hers, and never had been—not if he could talk to her that way.

This gut-wrenching grief was her fault, and there was no one to blame but herself. She was the one who'd got it backward. She'd surrendered her heart to Noah before he'd surrendered his to the Lord.

Beth spent Sunday morning on her balcony, lying on the sofa with an ice pack over her eyes, nursing the aftereffects of a crying jag. The swollen eyes and the headache would subside if she could stop the scene last night from playing over and over in her mind. Where had she gone wrong? Had she been too pushy, witnessing to Noah about the importance of a connection with the Lord?

On Monday, Noah didn't seem as angry, but he didn't smile once during the whole day, and he did remind her to work on his replacement.

On Tuesday, emotions ran a little high. Admittedly, she'd been too free with snippy comments, and Noah overplayed the role of subservient nurse. Vanessa looked anxious, but Mona seemed pleased. That evening, Beth confessed to Grandpa that Noah was leaving, and she would soon need two replacements. One could be Roxie Romandine, her nurse friend from New York who had family in L.A. and was ready to move. Grandpa said the other could be a nurse in Charlie's office who'd asked for a transfer.

On Wednesday, Beth didn't snip once, and Noah seemed more like himself. That evening she had dinner with Meg and Ry, who reminded her that even this suffering could be part of God's plan. Sunny called to say bad times could be God's preparation for the very best. Pete took the phone and backed Sunny up. The worst days of his life came right before the best.

On Thursday, Beth decided to take the offensive. She'd prayed herself into a better attitude, and she was just as loving and nice at work as she knew how to be. Vanessa said she was so relieved that she and Noah had made up.

That night Beth wore a dress for the Mother-Daughter Tea that was as different from her office uniform as it could possibly be. The black fabric clung to her figure almost too well, and the black high heels made her legs look long and shapely. How she dressed wouldn't change Noah's attitude, but surrendering to the possibilities meant she had to go outside her comfort level once in a while.

When she picked up Kendra, the little girl giggled and said, "Daddy looks so funny."

Beth turned to see what Kendra meant.

Noah's mouth lifted at one corner. "I think Kendi caught my reaction to…your outfit." His eyes scanned her length appreciatively. "You look amazing, Beth."

That appreciative look was worth all the trouble it had taken to dress up. "Thanks. I thought the outfit might be a little too dressy, but when a woman's taking the princess to a party, she's gotta go big or she'll look like the nanny."

"No one will mistake you for the nanny," he said dryly. "Not in that dress."

Maybe she would start wearing dresses more often.

Noah began watching for Beth and Kendi at eight o'clock. A little after nine, they arrived. He hustled out of the house, knowing Kendi would be asleep, and he didn't want Beth to carry the weight of his daughter. Kendi was probably getting too big to be carried inside, but he still loved doing it.

"The nanny-chauffeur has arrived," Beth said, nodding to her sleeping passenger.

"Did she make it through the party without nodding off?" Noah asked, unbuckling Kendra's seat belt.

"Actually, she did. Noah, she was adorable.

She told the people at our table about Chloe the Clown at Collin's wedding, about the promise rainbow she saw that day and all about my office decor."

He picked up his child and carried her inside. "So, you two had fun tonight?"

She nodded. "Lots of fun. Kendra says she wants us to go 'nex' year and ev'ry year.'"

That was a lot of pressure for Beth. "What did you tell her?"

"I answered generically, saying it was a wonderful party, but if it's okay with you, I'll take her until she grows up and has daughters of her own...or until you find someone who's easier to love than me."

"No one is easier to love, Beth." Why would she say a thing like that? She was the most lovable person he'd ever known. "Do you want to come in? Kendi loves it when you put her to bed."

"I don't think so," she said, not looking at him.

"We could talk."

"What about? Is anything different since we 'talked' Saturday night? I'm still a Brennan. You're still a 'giver, not a taker.' I still believe God has a plan. Unless you've come to believe that, too, what do we talk about?"

She was right. Nothing had changed. Why had he invited her in? Was it out of habit, or did he need her more than he wanted to admit? In the glow from the front-door light, she looked so beautiful. He would remember her this way.

"I love you, Noah."

Sensation rocketed through his mind. Had she really said that?

"I can't remember if I've said that or not, but I want you to know it. There's a love in my heart that I can't explain. Maybe God put it there. I don't know, but I *do* know it's not just for now...but forever."

Before he could think what to say, she had backed out of the driveway and driven away.

He carried Kendi to her bedroom, unbuttoned her yellow dress and helped her slip into her princess nightie, all of which she did without opening her eyes. He put her little toy animal in her hand, tucked her in and expected her to zonk out as usual. But she opened her eyes and reached one little hand toward him.

"Daddy?"

He knelt beside her bed. "What, puddin'?"

She stroked his cheek lovingly. "Daddy, you need a promise rainbow."

She closed her eyes, and she was dead asleep.

She was also dead right. He was a mess without Beth, and he needed the promise that God was in control. He went to his room and knelt by his bed.

Father God, I expect You've been waiting for me like I waited for Kendi to come home tonight. If she blew me off and disrespected me like I have You, it would break my heart. I'm on my knees, Lord, humbled by my own child's faith, asking You to forgive me.

I've been thinking a lot about what Beth said— about how I feel about Kendi and how You may feel about me. When Kendi doesn't get her way, she doesn't pout endlessly, but I've let doubt take over my life, and I've been denying You since Merrilee died.

Kendi knows I don't like it if she stays mad, and she needs my love so much that she changes her attitude. Why wasn't I like that with You, Father? In my grief, I should have turned to You. Instead I told myself You didn't care.

I didn't think You had a plan for me—although Your Word says You do. I guess that means I have to consider that Merrilee's death wasn't meaningless, and You still have a good future for Kendi and me.

I'm trying to figure out where I went wrong and when I started to doubt You about everything. I don't want to ever do that again. Lord, help me see You as Father and Friend. Help me trust You to lead the way. In Jesus' name, amen.

Noah held his hands out as a gesture of surrender and wept silently. He had so much to learn and a lot to make up for, but a comforting presence came over him. Whatever happened, everything would be okay.

Chapter Sixteen

Today would be her last day at Brennan Medical Clinic, but she didn't care anymore. There was no reason to stay. Keith wasn't coming back, and she might never see him again. The thought was too painful to bear.

She'd been a young, beautiful woman, fresh out of nursing school, when Keith hired her. He'd shared how lonely he was...not that he'd put it into words, but she'd seen for herself. And she'd been right.

On the day he found out that his wife couldn't bear children, who had he turned to? His pretty nurse, that's who, and late that afternoon, in his office, she'd given herself to Keith as she had to no other.

They'd only been together the one time—which he claimed to regret, but she hadn't—not even when she found she was carrying his child, her baby, their little son.

Keith had been wonderful. He'd given her the choice of raising the child with his financial support in a town far away to avoid scandal for the baby's sake or of letting Keith and his wife, Karen, adopt the baby.

She made her choice. She couldn't leave Keith. Letting her baby go was terrible, but she wasn't losing him for good. She would see him because she would see Keith. The weekends were lonely, but Keith was hers through the week.

When Karen died, she'd understood why Keith couldn't ask her to marry him. The Brennans had created such a hoity-toity climate at the clinic, the gossips would have accused them of carrying on for years. It would have ruined the purity of their love.

If it weren't for the Brennans, everything would have been different. She could have kept her baby. If the baby had been with her, he might have lived. If he'd lived, Keith would have married her. By now, they would have had grandchildren, and Keith wouldn't be where he was now.

Her only consolation was knowing the Brennans would suffer. Gossip was a powerful, vicious animal, and she'd unleashed it last night, calling as many parents as she could in one evening. She'd known she wouldn't have another chance, and she'd already emptied her desk of personal items.

The only reason to go to work today was to laugh in their faces. It was payback time. Bethie and the old coot were going down. They'd taken her man, but she'd taken their computer files—nothing recent, not with Noah, Vanessa or Beth always snooping—but she had medical information about the children of movie stars that the tabloids would pay for. The Brennans would be discredited and she would be set for life.

Today was going to be great! Noah could hardly wait to see Beth. He'd thought about calling her last night, but he didn't want there to be any confusion—in her mind or the Lord's—about the reason he'd given his heart back to God.

First and foremost, it was about his relationship with the Lord. He couldn't remember when he'd felt such joy. When he sang good morning to Kendi, he'd sung a children's church song with her, too. She'd smiled big and said, "Daddy, you're different!"

The differences were just beginning. It was still hard for him to believe that God wanted him to marry a Brennan, but if everything was going to be all right, it couldn't mean life without Beth.

He must have checked his watch a dozen times, impatient for her to arrive at the office, but she was really late and still might not be in for a while. A patient at the hospital had taken a turn for the worse. Her schedule was going to be too tight for them to talk during office hours. Could he hold his good news until late afternoon?

As expected, by the time she arrive, the lobby was full of patients. If she noticed that he was in an unusually good mood, she didn't comment on it. In fact, Beth seemed depressed, more so by the minute. Things must have gone badly for the patient.

It was almost lunch time when he took a phone call that put an end to his newfound peace. Boiling mad, he wanted to take care of the situation his way and now! If Beth didn't let Mona go after hearing this, if she wavered again, what should he do? Options ran through his mind…until he remembered to pray.

Lord, maybe this is a test of my trust in You and Your power. Please give Beth the guts to do what has to be done and the wisdom to do it.

Noah checked Beth's schedule, looking for the best time to drop the bombshell. She had a couple of patients to see before lunch. Should he wait until then? Maybe not.

"Can I see you for a minute?" he said, stepping inside the exam room as her last patient left to make an appointment with Vanessa.

Beth shut the door behind him and leaned against the exam table. "What's up?"

She looked so weary, he wished that what he had to say could wait. "I had a call from Stacee Drezek. Mona is calling your patients and *urging* them to find a new, more competent pediatrician because…get this…Dr. Crabtree is *not* coming back."

That seemed to shock her as much as it had him.

"Stacee and her friends thought it was weird when Mona called them the first time, insisting Keith *would* be back. This time, hearing her change her story, they think she's a psycho. They're not questioning your competence as a physician, but they wonder why Mona's working here."

Beth's shoulders slumped. "What did you tell Stacee?"

"I thanked her for the call, assured her you were extremely competent and said I'd tell you."

She dipped her head and turned slightly as if she didn't want him to see her reaction. "Thank you, Noah. I think we only have a couple of patients who are waiting. While I see them, I'll be praying about what to do."

"Beth! You have to let her go."

"I know! Mona will be going today. It's just that…" Her voice faltered. "This means you're leaving, too."

He hadn't thought of that. He'd said he would only stay until Mona was gone, he hadn't put his future in the hands of the Lord.

"If you want to remain working at the clinic, there's a nurse in Uncle Charlie's office who's interested in a transfer. Like you, I knew Mona would try something again, so I have a nurse friend from New York who'll be taking Mona's place. I hope you'll stay until Roxie settles in."

"No problem." He looked away, barely able to breathe with this rock in his chest. This isn't what he wanted, but it wasn't the time to say everything had changed. When would he have a chance to tell her, and would it make a difference when he did?

She left to see another patient, and they went through the motions, getting through the schedule efficiently. Beth didn't dally with her patients as she often did.

Mona and Vanessa were still up front when she asked him to follow her to her office. "I'm going to call Grandpa and have Human Resources walk me through the steps of Mona's dismissal," she said. "I'd like to do it right after lunch."

"Can I bring you something to eat?"

"I'm not hungry, but you go ahead."

"You might need me." Food was the last thing on his mind. How did he take back words spoken in anger, prompted by pride? "I'd like to stick around."

She placed her call to the chief and went about the business of setting up Mona's dismissal in her brisk, professional manner. Beth was getting the job done as she'd promised. If he were in her shoes, knowing that Mona was out to cause harm, could he have managed as well?

"It's set," she said, ending the call. "Grandpa's coming up. His office assistant will reschedule our afternoon patients while Vanessa and Mona are at lunch. A computer tech is on the way to see if files have been tampered with. A security guard will be here when Mona gets back from lunch. He'll stay with her while she carries the personal contents from her desk to the exit."

"Can I be here? It sounds like you have everything covered, but I don't trust Mona at all."

"Neither do I! I would be glad to have you here, but you shouldn't be in the room when a coworker is fired."

He should have thought of that himself.

"But you could stay close by, perhaps just outside the door? I'd like that."

"Then I'll be there."

"Would you excuse me for a few minutes, Noah?" she asked quietly. "I need a little time alone."

Did she want him out of her presence, or did she want time to pray? Probably both. If he hadn't taken so long to get right with God, he could have prayed with her.

"Maybe you could find a box for Mona's things," she said as he turned to leave. "I said I would clean out Mona's desk myself, and I will."

"I'll do that." It was the least he could do.

When Vanessa came back from lunch, the computer tech was already at work, and a security guard stood just out of sight by the door to the lobby.

Vanessa looked at Noah with big eyes. "Does this mean what I hope it means?" she whispered.

He nodded, though he didn't share her happy anticipation. Another day, he would have, but he dreaded what Beth had yet to go through.

Beth's grandfather walked in, nodded to them both and headed back to Beth's office. Noah sat at his desk and silently prayed.

Lord, I wish I could be there with Beth, but You'll be there, and that's even better. Help her, Lord. Keep her safe and strong.

Mona breezed through the door and put her purse away.

"Mona." The chief called from the end of the hall. "Would you join us?"

She looked at Vanessa and Noah with a gleam in her eyes before strutting down the hall. Over her shoulder, she said gaily, "Aren't you two coming to my retirement party?"

"She's crazy!" Vanessa said, looking scared.

"We aren't expecting any patients this afternoon," he said, "but let me know if someone shows up. I'll be outside Beth's office."

Beth leaned against her desk, ready to do what had to be done. Her grandfather patted her shoulder as he walked around the desk and sat in her chair. "We're going to get through this, darling," he said quietly, though he had the look of a warrior.

"What? No balloons and no cake?" Mona said as she came through the door. "I was hoping for cranberry punch."

"The most I can offer is a chair," Beth said, not really expecting Mona to sit. "Please, have a seat."

"Why? I won't be here long."

Beth turned to her grandfather and let him take the lead. He'd offered it to her, but she'd yielded to his greater experience. Besides, he'd known Mona for decades. He would know the right things to say.

"I'm thinking of the last time we talked, Mona," Grandpa said, lacing his fingers as he leaned back in the chair. "We offered you a handsome retirement package only a couple of months ago, yet you're here, obviously expecting this to be your last day. I'm curious. If you knew you were going to leave, why didn't you take the package?"

"The circumstances are different. Two months ago, I planned to be here when Keith returned."

Grandpa frowned. "He told you he would be back?"

"No, but I know you forced him out to make room for Beth. I knew he'd be back if she wasn't here, and I planned to make sure she wasn't. It was nothing personal, Beth," Mona said with a smirk.

It felt very personal. Mona's attitude was getting under Beth's skin. "My grandfather didn't force Keith to leave. That was his choice."

Mona shrugged. "So you *say*. What I *know* is that we'd seldom been apart, and Keith depended on me."

"You love him, don't you, Mona?" Grandpa sounded genuinely sympathetic. "You've loved him for years."

"Of course I love him."

"It must be horrible to love someone so much… and not have his love in return."

"But I did! I can't remember when Keith didn't

love me. You don't know anything! Did you know I carried his baby? Or that I let Keith and his wife adopt my son?"

Noah had mentioned a picture of a baby on Keith's credenza. That was her baby? How awful for Mona.

"As I remember, the child died of SIDS," Grandpa said.

Mona nodded, grief aging her face. "Keith and I got through it together."

"How long have you kept that secret, Mona?" Beth asked.

For a few seconds, Beth thought Mona wasn't going to answer, but she said with trembling lips, "In January, it will be thirty-three years."

Grandpa cleared his voice. "I'm sorry for your loss."

"I am, too," Beth said.

"Thank you," Mona said, shaking off her sadness. "But I don't think you've called me in here to offer condolences. Maybe I should be offering mine."

"That won't be necessary," Beth said. Mona may have made a dent in her credibility, but that's all it would be.

"As you apparently suspect," Grandpa said, "we've learned that you were quite active last night, calling parents and telling them Keith wouldn't be back. What made you do that, Mona?"

"I had to set the record straight. I'd personally assured them Keith *would* be back."

"What's convinced you now that he won't be?"

"I used my life's savings to hire an investigator," Mona said, her lip curled. "He found Keith living on property purchased *years* ago. It's in the South Pacific—one of the Fiji islands, to be exact. Did you know that?"

Beth nodded.

"You knew?" Mona exclaimed, her eyes blazing. "All those fishing trips—you knew that's where he was going?"

"I did," Grandpa said.

Her face contorted in malevolent rage. "Did you know his island housekeeper is now *Mrs. Crabtree*?"

"No, I didn't know that," Grandpa said. The lines between his brow deepened.

"Isn't that a joke?" Her laugh was almost a sob.

"A joke?" Grandpa asked. "I'm afraid I don't get it."

"But it's so funny. I was good enough to be Keith's nurse and good enough to be the mother of his child, but, when his wife died and he could have married me, I wasn't good enough to be his wife. Yet, this island woman with no education, no social standing, nothing worthy of being Mrs. Keith Crabtree—*she's* good enough. If that's not funny, what is?"

Beth was so appalled at Mona's thinking, she could only stare.

"'Good enough'?" Grandpa repeated, shaking his head in amazement. "It's been a while since I heard that. Mona, money and social position aren't the measure of a person—not the way they used to be. It still exists in the minds of small-minded people, but it's what you *do* with your life that counts. It's not what you *have* or where you came from."

"That's what I should expect you to say," she said, just as angry as ever. "Defend Keith. But you and this clinic have robbed me of my life."

Grandpa threw up his hands.

Beth understood. There was no reasoning with a woman this delusional.

"So, what happens now?" he asked. "You've wasted your life and your savings on a man who didn't deserve you, and he's cost you your job."

"I'm not without resources," she said with a smirk. "The things I know are worth money."

Grandpa leaned forward. "If you've taken information from this office," he said in a low, ominous tone, "or if you reveal anything you came to know while working here, it's not going to earn you one dime. I'll make sure you are prosecuted to the full extent of the law for violating privacy issues and stealing company information. You'll end up in jail or in poverty. Either way, it's not a pretty picture."

Beth felt a jolt of adrenaline at the threat in his voice. There was no mistaking he meant what he said.

For the first time, Mona seemed uncertain.

"But," Grandpa said, leaning back in his chair with a sigh, "my granddaughter wants to offer you a better future. She has this thing about wanting to show God's love. So, here's what we're going to do…."

Noah stood by the door as Beth had asked him to do, listening to her grandfather offer Mona retirement benefits on the condition that she provide the information to right the wrongs she'd done to Beth and the clinic.

If Mona had spat in the chief's face, it wouldn't have surprised Noah, but he was almost sure he heard her softly crying. He didn't know what surprised him more: that Mona had finally caved, that Beth still wanted to show love to Mona or that the chief had been so clear that the measure of a person wasn't what he had, but how he lived his life.

Noah was back at his desk when Mona, Beth

and the chief emerged minutes later. He looked directly at Beth, silently asking if she was okay.

She nodded, but he could see that the meeting had taken its toll.

When she went back to her office and Mona left with the chief and the guard, Noah told Vanessa he was going to lunch. He still wasn't hungry, but he needed a few minutes to think about what had just happened.

Outside the clinic cafeteria, he sat on the patio, sipped iced tea, listened to the splashing of the garden fountain and prayed. *God, help me think this through.*

If he was any kind of man at all, he had to consider what he'd heard the chief say about "good enough."

Noah had grown up in circumstances where others thought he wasn't good enough, but he didn't think that of himself. People who had more money, were better educated or came from a different background weren't better, and he wasn't less because they had more.

But if he really believed that, why had he run from the best thing that ever happened to him? Was he that afraid of what people would say about him marrying a Brennan? What man in his right mind would forfeit the woman he loved to prove—and that's what it was, a prideful need to prove—that he was good enough? That made him as pitiful as Mona.

If his faith was real, if he'd meant what he told the Lord, then all doubts—all worries and fears—belonged to the One with ultimate control. Beth said she loved him…that she would love him forever. He didn't understand how she could, but if she wanted his love, it was hers. No one would ever love her more.

But how could she love him after the hurtful things he'd said and done? If he could undo them, he would. She deserved to know that, and there was no better time than now. He would start with an apology, but what then?

Lord, do I tell Beth I love her or start with the news that I've come back to You?

"Beth?" Noah said with a tap on her door.

She called for him to come in, praying that she wouldn't be like Mona, holding on to her one-sided love.

He shut the door behind him and walked slowly toward her. A muscle twitched in his jaw, and his eyes had the intense look of a man who had something to say, but didn't know how to say it. She should help him.

"I just got off the phone with Roxie Romandine in New York," she said, trying to sound upbeat.

"She'll be in the office Wednesday. If you want the transfer to Uncle Charlie's office, you could begin there Thursday morning."

He winced as if she'd struck him. "I'm not interested in working in your uncle's office."

He wanted no part of her *and* her family?

He sat on the edge of her desk as he had so many times before, supporting himself with that strong arm she so admired. She faked a reassuring smile. They would get through this, and then get on with life.

"Beth, I wanted to tell you something this morning, but there was never a chance. Last night after you dropped Kendi off, I got on my knees for the first time in a long while. I told the Lord I was sorry for ignoring Him, and it would never happen again."

"Noah! That's wonderful!" She could hardly believe it. It was far from what she'd expected to hear, and so much better!

"I wanted to tell you as soon as I saw you this morning, but the day got crazy. After you left last night, I knew I had to make things right with God, or at least try. The amazing thing was I felt His presence, Beth. I knew He was listening. Whatever happens about anything else, I'll owe you forever. Watching you love the Lord made me want to have Him back in my life."

That made her love him even more. There was contentment in his eyes that she'd never seen before, but she recognized it. It came with knowing the Lord.

"I don't know how you can forgive me for being so rude the other night. You didn't deserve any of that attitude or those awful words. I'm so sorry, Beth."

"But wasn't that a different man talking?" She smiled to let him know he needn't worry.

"Very different," he agreed. His eyes moved over every inch of her face and stopped on her mouth.

Hope exploded in her heart. It wasn't over if he could look at her like that.

He took a step closer. "Beth, if you'll give me another chance, I'll—"

She'd heard all she needed to hear. It only took one spectacular effort to get out of her chair and into his arms, the best place on earth. He held her high, her feet off the floor, and claimed kisses that were long overdue. The feel of his mouth on hers and his arms around her was all she had hoped for.

He buried his face in her neck and murmured, "I love you, Beth, and I need you."

She leaned back to look in his eyes, his beautiful eyes, so filled with love.

"I can hardly believe I said that. From the time I was a kid I never admitted that I needed anybody, but it's the truth. Beth, I need you."

"I need you, too," she said, caressing his face. "I know you said you would only stay until—"

"I'm not going anywhere! If you'll have me, I'm yours every day for the rest of my life."

There just weren't words to match that. She wrapped her arms around him even tighter and let her kiss say he belonged to her. That was a promise forever.

"Do we have to have a big Brennan wedding?" he asked softly, his mouth near hers.

That was the last thing she wanted. "If you aren't concerned about the details of where we'll live and all that, I'll marry you tonight…"

His coffee-colored eyes lit up at the thought.

"But tonight *is* pizza night," she teased, "and we shouldn't miss that."

"You know that Kendi's going to be flying high as a kite, don't you?" he said with a grin.

"She won't be the only one. I think Grandpa's going to be just as happy."

His eyes roved her face, looking at her with all the love any woman could ask for. "It's your call, Beth. Do we elope and begin our life today or do we take time before making a lifetime commitment?"

"Will you be upset if I say I'd like to pray about it?"

"No," he said, smiling. "But I wish I'd thought of it first. It's my turn to pray."

With her arms around Noah and her head on his chest, Beth marveled at Noah's words of surrender. This joy of being in the arms of the man she loved while he talked to the Lord…it was all she had prayed for…and more.

Epilogue

Three years later

"Okay, guys, you look a lot alike, but I know which one is which, and I'm telling if you cry. I'm supposed to. I'm in charge. You're the first real babies I've ever been in charge of. You're very cute, both of you.

"I'm only ten, and even though you're really little, I can't walk you around unless you're in your stroller. But if you lay here nice on the blanket, I'll sit with you as long as you stay awake.

"That won't be long, so I'd better hurry up and tell you the rest of the story.

"Mom and Daddy didn't get married that day, but they did get married the next week! It wasn't like a regular wedding, like in a church.

"The preacher was there, but the wedding was on the beach in back of Pete and Sunny's house. All of us took off our shoes and walked across the sand to stand by the ocean. Except for Harlene. With her bunions, she needed her special shoes.

"There were chairs for her and Grandpa, but everyone else stood—Uncle Ry and Auntie Meg, Pete and Sunny and their kids, the preacher and his wife, Mom and Daddy and me. I got to stand between Mom and Daddy, and I held the rainbow kite. There had to be a promise rainbow for the wedding.

"Pete cooked hamburgers and corn on the cob. I told you it wasn't a regular wedding. We talked about how Mom and Daddy fell in love. Grandpa got a present because he was the one who introduced them. Harlene got a present because, when she got sick, that's when they started to fall in love. I got a present because I begged Daddy to ask Mom to pizza night.

"Mom told Grandpa she was sorry because she wasn't going to be Dr. Brennan anymore, but Daddy said she could use her old name and her new name if she put a little line in between. That's called a hyphen. You learn stuff like that when you're ten.

"Mom said she would love to be Dr. Brennan-McKnight. She wanted the same name as me 'cause I was gonna be her daughter as soon as the judge said. But I knew she was my mom when we shopped for the yellow dress.

"Daddy helped me put Mommy Merrilee's pictures in a book, all but one for my room. We talked about how nice it was of God to give me two mommies. I decided Merrilee would be my mommy, and Beth would be my mom.

"She's a really, really good mom, guys. You're gonna love her so much! And our daddy is the best dad!

"You look a little bit like him. Mom says a lot. I don't know. You got his color of eyes and hair, but I don't think he was ever as little as you.

"Daddy found us this house, and Mom said she was proud of him for thinking outside the box. Wasn't that a funny thing to say?

"We moved in when Mom and Daddy got back from their honeymoon. While they were gone, I stayed with my new grandpa. I'd never had a grandpa before. He got me a doctor kit like Mom had when she was a little girl, and he pretended to be sick so I could be his doctor. I think that's what I'm gonna be when I grow up—a doctor.

"I'm sorry you guys won't get to meet Grandpa, not until you're old and go to heaven. That's where he is now…with my mommy.

"We have a really big house, guys. We even

have a grandparent suite, which is like an apartment, and it's for Harlene. She cried when we asked her to move with us to the new house, but we told her she was our family.

"When you get bigger, you each get your own room like me, and we have an extra bedroom besides the one for Mom and Daddy. We've got our own swings and lots of stuff like a park! And we have our own swimming pool!

"There's somebody new to take care of you guys while Mom and Daddy are at work. Harlene is a very good babysitter for big kids like me, but babies need a nanny.

"Your new nanny is Vanessa's mother, Teresa. She stayed with Harlene and me while Mom and Daddy were at the hospital with you two. Teresa's great! You're gonna like her so much!

"Teresa asked Mom if she was disappointed you were both boys, but Mom said she already had the best little daughter a mother could ask for.

"That's me! Your big sister—Kendra!"

* * * * *

Dear Reader,

If this story touched your heart or if you smiled once in a while, the credit belongs to the Lord. Ideas for the story came out of nowhere—or that's what we say when we forget that we've prayed for those very ideas.

The starting point was Beth Brennan, a pediatrician in my Love Inspired novel, *Man of Her Dreams* (February 2005). I thought she should have a male office nurse, and, for no particular reason—or so I thought—I named him Noah. With his name came the promise of a rainbow and the assurance that God has everything under control.

Like Noah, I was raised by a grandparent. When my mother died at Merrilee's age, Granny Beth adopted me and lived to see me loved by my precious family. It's always been difficult to see God as my Father because, like Beth, I didn't have a good dad. When she compares Noah's feelings for his daughter to God's feeling for Noah—that was for me.

In this story, Kendra is very much like our granddaughter—the real Kendra who loves yellow as much as she likes to be in charge. Her parents were a big help with the story, and other parents, like Terry Logan, contributed, too.

If you're interested in still more personal stuff, please visit my Web site, www.pattmarr.com. You can e-mail me there, or write to me at P.O. Box 13, Silvis, IL, 61282. Hearing from you is such an encouragement that I answer every note. Tell me something about yourself, what you like to read or what you want me to pray about.

In Him,

Patt Marr

QUESTIONS FOR DISCUSSION

1. Compared to her family, Beth considers herself to be eccentric (her yellow sneakers; her yellow "bugster"). What made her decide to do things her own way? Have you ever experienced a family situation you wanted to run from?

2. When Beth met Noah, his faith had been challenged by his wife's death. If he had not regained his faith, should Beth have married him? Have you seen marriages that started with a difference in faith? What happens when a couple shares the same faith but later one or both of them changes?

3. As a single parent, Noah struggles to keep his daughter from caring too much for Beth. Should Noah have protected Kendra in that fashion, or should he have been glad his child was being loved, regardless of the nature of the relationship between him and Beth?

4. Beth is mistreated by her brother, Trey. Is it possible to have a loving relationship with a difficult parent or sibling? When, if ever, does a Christian say, "Enough," and move out of the line of family anger?

5. Have you ever had a coworker as difficult to work with as nurse Mona? Were you as long-suffering as Beth? Should Beth have given up sooner?

6.   Noah believes Beth is out of his league and that he isn't good enough because of his background. Have you felt that way? Does being a Christian take that feeling away? Does it return and sweep over you like a huge unexpected wave? If it does, what brings you back to safety?

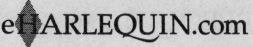